❖ Toy Dance Party ❖

TOY DANCE PARTY

✤

BEING THE FURTHER ADVENTURES

OF A BOSSYBOOTS STINGRAY,

A COURAGEOUS BUFFALO,

AND A HOPEFUL ROUND SOMEONE CALLED PLASTIC

✤

EMILY JENKINS

ILLUSTRATED BY PAUL O. ZELINSKY

✤

schwartz & wade books · new york

Published by Schwartz & Wade Books
an imprint of Random House Children's Books
a division of Random House, Inc.
New York

Visit us on the Web! www.randomhouse.com/kids
Educators and librarians, for a variety of teaching tools, visit us at
www.randomhouse.com/teachers

Library of Congress Cataloging-in-Publication Data
Jenkins, Emily.
Toy dance party : being the further adventures of a bossyboots Stingray, a courageous
Buffalo, and a hopeful round someone called Plastic / Emily Jenkins ; illustrated by Paul O.
Zelinsky. — 1st ed.
p.   cm.
Summary: Six stories relate further adventures of three best friends, who happen to be toys,
as they encounter a fearsome (possible) shark, enjoy a dance party, and deal with rejection by
The Girl, who is growing up.
Contents: The toys are left in—In which there are wonderful costumes and violence
occurs—The garbage-eating shark (which is not the same as the possible shark)—
Concerning that plump mouse Bonkers, the vacuum cleaner, and a friendship between fish—
In which there is a sleepover and somebody needs repair—Let's do our nails.
ISBN 978-0-375-83935-1 (hardcover)—ISBN 978-0-375-93935-8 (Gibraltar lib. bdg.)
[1. Toys—Fiction.   2. Best friends—Fiction.   3. Friendship—Fiction.   4. Adventure and
adventurers—Fiction.]   I. Zelinsky, Paul O., ill.   II. Title.

PZ7.J4134Tov 2008
[E]—dc22
2007044112

The text of this book is set in 13-point Archetype.
Printed in the United States of America
10 9 8 7 6 5 4 3 2 1
First Edition

In loving memory of Joan R. Carey

—E.J.

In memory of Bernie, whose wife loves toys

—P.Z.

CONTENTS

✣

❧ TOY DANCE PARTY ❧

CHAPTER ONE

✤

The Toys Are Left In

Lumphy, the stuffed buffalo, did not go with the Girl on winter vacation.

StingRay did not go, either. She thought she would. The Girl even told her she would, because she and StingRay sleep together, every single night, on the high bed with the fluffy pillows. But in the end, when the suitcases were packed and the car loaded, the Girl and her parents drove away—and StingRay was left behind.

Plastic, being only a ball, had not expected to go on the trip. No one plays with balls in snowy weather. She is here with StingRay and Lumphy in the empty house, finding it strange to have days go by without the good-natured ruckus of the people who live there. No alarm clocks, no morning bustle, no baths, no cooking smells. No laughter, no arguments, no stories read aloud.

The house is cold.

For several days—they are not sure how many—Lumphy, StingRay, and Plastic play checkers and Hungry Hungry Hippos with the toy mice and the one-eared sheep. They chat with the rocking horse in the corner and with TukTuk, the old yellow towel in the hallway bathroom. They watch television. But the hours go by much more slowly than usual. There is always the feeling of someone missing. The Girl they love.

"When is she coming back, again?" Plastic wonders one afternoon. She and Lumphy are on the windowsill, downstairs in the living room. Lumphy is watching the

snow falling outside, and Plastic has been reading a book about cheese—kinds of cheese, where it comes from, and how it's made. She is flipping the pages herself with a rolling technique she's invented.

"The Saturday before school starts again, is what they said," Lumphy answers. He feels sick to his stomach when he thinks about how the Girl isn't here.

"What Saturday is that?" Plastic asks.

"I don't know. A week is how long they'll be gone."

"But how long is a week?" Plastic persists.

"StingRay says five days."

"What day is it now?" wonders Plastic. "Is it Tuesday? I think it's maybe Tuesday." She rocks anxiously from side to side.

"Urmph," mumbles Lumphy. He is counting in his head.

"What are the days besides Tuesday, anyhow?" continues Plastic. "Does it go Onesday, Tuesday, Threesday, Foursday?"

"I think they have already been gone *more* than five days," announces Lumphy.

"You mean we already had Tuesday?"

"I mean we already had *Saturday*," says Lumphy. "I mean, the week is up."

Fwap! Gobble-a gobble-a.

Fwap! Gobble-a gobble-a.

They are interrupted.

Fwap! Gobble-a gobble-a.

StingRay is falling down the stairs. Flipper over plush flipper, bouncing first off the wall, then off the posts beneath the banister.

Fwap! Gobble-a gobble-a.

Fwap! Gobble-a gobble-a. And then eventually: Bonk! She lands at the bottom.

Lumphy climbs gingerly off the windowsill while Plastic bounces over to StingRay. "Are you okay?"

StingRay is lying on her back, and her head hurts where she banged it on a post, but she quickly turns over on her tummy and brushes her eye with her left flipper. "What do you mean?"

"You fell down the stairs."

"I don't know what you're talking about. I come down that way all the time on purpose." StingRay changes the subject. "What have you been doing?"

"I was reading!" Plastic tells her. "Did you know cheese is made in caves? Because it is! You put milk in a cave and out comes cheese!"

"Of course I knew that," says StingRay, although she didn't. "Listen. Do you know where the playing cards are? I can't find them anywhere and I want to play Fish."

Plastic and Lumphy agree to help look for the cards. They search the downstairs, checking bookshelves and the drawers of the coffee table—but the cards are not there. They go upstairs: Lumphy climbing, StingRay lurching up each step with a strong push of her tail, and Plastic bouncing easily, five stairs at a time.

They look through the Girl's bedroom again. Search

under the high bed. Look behind the box that holds the board games.

Then they realize: the Girl has packed the cards. She has taken them with her on vacation, where she has not taken Lumphy, or Plastic, or StingRay.

"What else has she packed?" cries StingRay, frantic. She flops herself across the bedroom carpet. "Did she pack that book about the mouse in the dungeon?"

Plastic takes a high bounce to look on the bedside table. "It's not here."

"Now we'll never find out what happens!" moans StingRay. "What else did she pack?"

Their survey reveals that the Girl has packed not only the book about the mouse in the dungeon *and* the deck of cards but

a box of dominoes,

a carton of LEGOs,

a paint box and a pad of art paper,

a jigsaw puzzle of a triceratops,

two Barbie dolls that don't talk and

never have,

and a vinyl box of Barbie outfits.

"Oh no!" StingRay cries when Plastic and Lumphy present her with the total. "Why did she take all the second-rate toys and leave us?"

"There, there," says Plastic. "She just . . ."

"She just what? She just forgot us, that's what! Forgot us and took those Barbie dolls who don't even say anything at all!"

"Maybe she went to a place that was good for Barbies," says Plastic. "Some kind of special Barbie place, where stingrays would get bored."

"Oh yeah?" StingRay throws herself on the carpet in distress. "And she needs her paint box there?

And her *dominoes*?

She hardly even likes the dominoes.

She never does puzzles!

She doesn't love me!

She's left me!"

"She's coming back," says Plastic. "She's coming back on Saturday." She doesn't tell StingRay what Lumphy told her—that maybe Saturday is already over.

"By Saturday she'll have forgotten all about us!" cries StingRay. Now she is twisting over and back on the carpet, gasping and sobbing.

And sobbing some more.

And even more sobbing.

This can't go on, thinks Lumphy. He has to do something.

He galumphs down the hall to the bathroom and grabs TukTuk, the faded yellow towel that hangs over the rack. Holding her corner in his mouth, he drags her as fast as he can into the Girl's bedroom, where StingRay is tossing and flopping. With one big motion, Lumphy throws TukTuk on top of StingRay, covering her eyes, her flippers, her whole body.

"Where are the lights?" StingRay yells.

It's all yellow in here!

I'm going blind.

I'll never see another sunrise.

Lumphy will have to lead me around

so I don't bump into furniture!"

StingRay is still twisting and crying, but the weight of TukTuk is such that she can no longer flip over. Lumphy backs up a couple of feet, and—rumpa lumpa, rumpa lumpa—jumps heavily onto TukTuk.

"Oh, umph!" cries StingRay. "You're on me, someone.

Someone's on me!

Someone heavy!

Oh heavens!

I knew it would come to this, some horrible day.

No one loves me!

I'm being squished!

I'm blind and my friends are squishing me!"

Lumphy sits. He sits on TukTuk, who lies on StingRay, and together they calm her down, resting on her so she feels their weight.

The sobbing stops.

She is barely moving now. One flipper is just thumping up and down.

Finally, StingRay is peaceful.

Lumphy climbs down from her broad plush back and pulls TukTuk behind him. "The Girl still loves us," he says.

"Okay," says StingRay meekly. "I just got concerned for a minute."

. . . . .

Half an hour later, all three toys are sitting on the windowsill in the living room. The snow is still coming down. Plastic is reading about cheese some more. StingRay is drawing shapes in the frost on the windowpane. And Lumphy is worrying.

"The Girl hasn't been here for a really, really long time," he says, breaking the silence.

"Where is she, again?" asks Plastic.

"Bolling. They said they were going to Bolling to see the grandpa."

"But where is Bolling?"

Lumphy does not answer.

"And *what* is Bolling?" wonders Plastic. "Is it a town, a hotel, a magical land, or what?"

Lumphy doesn't answer, because he doesn't know. "It has been more than five days," he says. "In fact, it has been *way* more than five days, and when it is more days than it is supposed to be, that means maybe the people are lost."

"Oh oh oh!" cries StingRay, suddenly afraid. "She loves us but she's lost!"

"Maybe everything is fine," Plastic says. "The Girl is just having fun in Bolling."

"We can *not* panic." Lumphy looks pointedly at

StingRay. "And we cannot pretend anymore." Looking now at Plastic: "I think something has gone wrong. I think the Girl is lost."

StingRay tries not to panic and makes a small noise like this: Frrrrrr, frrrrrr.

"I have to go outside and look for her," announces Lumphy. "The Girl needs me."

"Is that a good idea?" asks StingRay. Frrrrrr, frrrrrr.

"Yes," says Lumphy. "I have to be tough and brave. We *all* have to be tough and brave."

Plastic bounces softly and whispers, "Brave, brave, brave!" to herself. Lumphy jumps off the windowsill and scurries to the kitchen. Plastic and StingRay follow more slowly.

"If I were lost, I know she would look for me," Lumphy tells them.

"Hello," says StingRay, following Lumphy to a cupboard, which he begins to pry open. "They went in the *car*. Bolling might be really far away."

"But they *could* be nearby," answers Lumphy.

"Won't we get wet?" StingRay is dry clean only. "Snow looks very wet." Frrrrrr, frrrrrr.

"We can't just stay home and not try to save her." Lumphy is determined. He gets a laminated place mat from the low cupboard. It has a baby stegosaurus on it. "I am a buffalo! I have thick woolly fur!" He stands on his hind legs and waves the place mat heroically over his head. "*You* don't have to get wet. *I* can save the Girl."

"How will you save her with woolly fur and a baby stegosaurus place mat?" asks StingRay.

Lumphy returns to the sill and opens the window with his forepaws. Icy air gusts into the room. Lumphy drops the place mat out the window onto a drift of snow and leaps after it. "It's a sled!" he calls as he lands squarely on the place mat and zips down the drift into the yard. "Wheee!"

Plastic and StingRay are watching him from the sill. A few feet from the house, the place mat comes to a stop.

"Now what?" calls Plastic.

"I'm going to try to find her!" says Lumphy, his voice sounding small in the blizzard.

"Go, go, go!" yells Plastic.

Lumphy wags his tail stump bravely. (He had a tail once, a good-looking chocolate-colored one; but now there is only a stump.) He squints his eyes against the storm and jumps off the place mat.

Slurrsh! He sinks into more than a foot of snow.

It is so, so cold. Lumphy did not realize it would be this cold.

It is colder, even, than the time that toddler came over and put Lumphy in the fridge for two hours.

Lumphy scrambles around with his forelegs and kicks with his back legs, reaching for the baby stegosaurus place mat and desperately trying to pull himself out of the hole.

But the snow is soft and he digs himself down deeper, until his tail stump feels the hard dirt of the frozen lawn beneath it.

"I knew you shouldn't go outside like that!" calls StingRay from the window. "I told you it was a bad idea."

Lumphy struggles some more, but his paws can't grasp the now slippery baby stegosaurus place mat. "I'm stuck!" he cries.

"Don't panic!" yells Plastic, remembering what Lumphy himself told StingRay.

"I need to rescue the Girl!" cries Lumphy, frantic at the thought of his own failure. The snow is drifting down and flakes are melting on his woolly buffalo fur.

"We're getting a spatula!" yells Plastic. Then, to StingRay: "Get a spatula."

"How are you going to save him with a spatula?" asks StingRay.

"Yeah, how?" moans Lumphy from his hole of snow.

"And what about the Girl? She needs me!" He is still try-ing to climb out.

"*I'm* not saving him with a spatula," Plastic tells StingRay. "*You* are." StingRay has never heard Plastic talk like this before. It is very bossy, and StingRay is not sure she likes to be bossed. But Lumphy is her best friend, so she follows Plastic to the kitchen. Together, they push a chair over to the counter. StingRay climbs the chair, heaves herself onto the tile, and looks at the jar full of wooden spoons, whisks, and spatulas.

"The kind of spatula for flipping pancakes, or the kind of spatula for scraping bowls?" she asks Plastic.

"Bowls!" says Plastic, bouncing high once to see what StingRay is talking about.

StingRay seizes a bowl-scraping spatula and leaps off the counter to the floor. "Now what?"

"Now you ride on the diplodocus place mat, then dig him out with the spatula," says Plastic, rolling over to the cupboard where the place mats are kept.

Fear crests over StingRay. "But I'm dry clean only," she says. Frrrrrr, frrrrrr.

"Dig, dig, dig!" cries Plastic.

"Can't *you* go out?" asks StingRay. "You're rubber. You like to get wet."

Plastic looks at StingRay, hard. Even though she doesn't have eyes. "I can't hold the spatula," she finally says.

It takes StingRay some effort to get the spatula and the diplodocus place mat up to the windowsill, and when she does, she is startled to see that quite a lot of snow has blown into the living room, through the open window. Night is falling, and the yard outside looks bleak and gray.

"StingRay, help!" cries Lumphy.

"She's coming, Lumphy!" yells Plastic. "She's coming with a spatula!"

As the buffalo did before her, StingRay drops her place mat onto the pile of snow at the edge of the house, then hurls herself out to land on it, squeezing the spatula under one flipper.

Zzzzuuushh! The diplodocus place mat skids through the yard toward the hole where Lumphy is stuck. StingRay is lucky and arrives quite near Lumphy, so she is able to poke her nose into the hole and see how he is doing.

Lumphy is very, very cold and sick to his stomach, but as soon as he sees his friend he stretches his body to touch his buffalo nose to hers.

"I am not panicking," says StingRay proudly. "I am being tough and brave!"

"That's good," says Lumphy. "Because *my* tough and brave turned out dumb."

StingRay brandishes her spatula. "I'm digging you out!" She rears up on her tail and jumps off the diplodocus place mat so she can dig.

Slurrsh!

She sinks.

She turns and tries to launch herself back onto the place mat, realizing her mistake, but the mat is slick with snow, and she can't get onto it. She flails around with the spatula, but that only makes her hole bigger.

"Help! Help! Oh!" she sobs. "I'm panicking now! I can't help it!" She struggles until the snow on one side of her hole collapses into Lumphy's hole and the two of them are together, surrounded by walls of powdery white.

There is nothing for them to do. Nothing they *can* do.

They will have to wait until the storm ends and the snow melts.

Frrrrrr, frrrrrr.

When her panicky feeling calms down, StingRay puts her flipper across Lumphy's cold back. The two of them hold on to each other in the snow.

Plastic watches from the window. There is no one else who can help. Sheep is on wheels, the toy mice are too small, and the rocking horse in the corner can't move around. Plastic stands watch for many hours as the snow floats into the hole where her friends are. At some point, she remembers that the lights are supposed to go off and bounces sadly at all the light switches until the house is once again in darkness.

. . . . .

Late that night, a car pulls into the driveway. Plastic hears a shuffling sound outside the front door. Then the voice of the Girl's dad. A jingle of keys. The porch light goes on.

The door opens, and the dad walks in, dragging a duffel bag. He shuts the open window, knocking Plastic to the floor, where she rolls until she bangs into the coffee table.

The people are home.

It is Saturday! The toys haven't missed it after all. Plastic can hardly keep herself from bouncing with relief.

The mom comes inside, too—but the Girl stops in the driveway and looks into the yard. There is a spatula there, in the light from the porch. And two dinosaur place mats.

Seconds later, she is lifting StingRay and Lumphy into her warm arms.

"Lumphy! You sweetie buffalo!" she cries. "Are you okay?" And "StingRay, you're all soggy! Did you fall out of my bag when we left the house? Let me take you inside."

She runs indoors with them, scooping up Plastic on the way to the bedroom. She rubs a frozen Lumphy and a soggy StingRay with TukTuk and sets them on the warming-up radiator to dry overnight, clucking and *tsk-*ing and being a good doctor. She makes sure they are safe, then goes over to give the rocking horse in the corner a kiss on the forehead. She squeezes Plastic and lies on her stomach to see the smaller toys, who are huddled together on a low shelf. "Hello, Sheep! Hello, Bonkers and Millie." She picks up each toy mouse in turn. "Hello, Brownie. Oh, and hello, Rocky. Can't forget *you*!"

On top of the radiator, Lumphy nudges StingRay. "You okay?"

"I'm okay," she whispers.

He waits for her to ask if *he's* okay, but she doesn't. That is StingRay's way. Finally, he says: "That was a dumb idea to go outside, huh?"

"Probably."

"I'm a dumb buffalo."

"You're a tough and brave buffalo," says StingRay. "It's just, that blizzard was so, so big."

"You think so?" he asks. "You think I'm brave?"

"I do," she tells him.

And everything is good again, because the Girl has come home.

CHAPTER TWO

⚜

In Which There Are Wonderful Costumes and Violence Occurs

The next morning, when the family is downstairs in the kitchen, Plastic rolls over to where Lumphy and StingRay are still drying on the radiator.

"I didn't know the toy mice had names," she whispers to her friends. "Did you?"

Lumphy didn't.

"I've been calling them Mice. Or just Mouse if there was only one," says Plastic.

"Me too," confesses Lumphy. "Just 'Hey there, Mouse. Come here, Mice.' Like that."

"Do you think they're mad?" worries Plastic.

"How could they be?" sniffs StingRay. "They're only mice."

"But we didn't know their names!" cries Plastic.

"Speak for yourself." StingRay flips over to get the warm radiator heat on her back. "I knew."

"You did? Did you know what their names *were*?"

"Um . . ." StingRay wavers. "Not exactly. But I knew they had nice mouselike names, just like they do. Like Bonko. That's precisely the kind of name I thought she'd have."

"Ahem," coughs Plastic.

"What ahem?"

"Bonk*ers*," corrects Plastic. "It's Bonk*ers*. Not Bonko."

"Whatever," sniffs StingRay. "I knew she had a name, is what I'm saying."

"He," says Plastic.

"What?"

"That plump mouse Bonkers is a he."

"How can you tell?" asks StingRay.

"He told me." Plastic bounces once, lightly.

Lumphy shakes his head, reflecting. "I thought they were all called Mouse. Like StingRay is called StingRay and Sheep is Sheep."

"And Rocking Horse is Rocking Horse," adds StingRay.

"Ahem," coughs Plastic.

"What now?" StingRay is irritated.

Plastic explains: "The horse is called Highlander. I thought everybody knew that."

"Well, do you know the Girl's name, then?" harrumphs StingRay, to cover her embarrassment. "Do you, huh?"

"Yeah," says Plastic.

"Yeah? You mean you know it?"

"Sure." Plastic twirls in self-satisfaction.

"What is it?" StingRay is too curious to pretend anymore.

"Honey," replies Plastic. "That's what her mom and dad call her when they wake her. They say, 'Get up, Honey. Good morning.' "

. . . . .

Honey charges up the stairs and everyone goes quiet. She shoves her feet into her winter boots and grabs a sweater from a drawer. "Can I take a Barbie?" she yells down the stairs.

Her mother sighs from below. "Why do you need a Barbie at the movies?"

"Just for fun. In the car," Honey answers.

StingRay wants to go to the movies.

StingRay wants to have fun in the car.

Why should a silent Barbie get to go when a knowledgeable and beautifully blue StingRay is available instead?

While Honey's back is turned, StingRay leaps off the radiator and scoots herself as close to the vinyl Barbie box as possible. She tries to look adorable.

"Fine," the mother calls. "But be quick. I don't have time for you to put it in a new outfit or anything. The movie starts at eleven-forty-five."

Honey puts on her sweater and walks over to the Barbie box. There is StingRay on the floor, looking up with those big eyes. "StingRay wants to go to the movies, too," Honey yells down the stairs. "She's never been."

"StingRay *or* a Barbie," her mother answers. "Not both."

"But I want to take StingRay."

"So leave the Barbie," says her mother. "Let's go."

Honey grabs StingRay, clips a barrette in her hair, and—ha *ha!* StingRay is off to the movies, and the Barbie box remains unopened.

. . . . .

When StingRay returns, she is glowing with happiness. Three hours alone with Honey! Three hours of specialness! Specialness forever and ever!

But instead of playing with StingRay, or reading to StingRay, or cuddling StingRay and talking about how wonderful it was going to the movies together, Honey tosses StingRay on the bed, grabs her old library books, and leaves the house with her parents. The toys are alone again.

The specialness is over.

"Plastic!" StingRay calls, pointing a flipper. "Come here. I have a new game to play."

Plastic rolls over to her.

"I will be Princess DaisySparkle," StingRay announces. "And you can be my ugly fairy pet."

"Okay, I'll be a fairy." Plastic bounces up to join StingRay on the high bed. "My name is . . . um . . . my name is Dimple!"

StingRay crinkles her nose. "No, your name has to be Wiggy. Wiggy is DaisySparkle's pet fairy."

"How about Pimple?" offers Plastic. "Or Plumcake? Or Pancake?"

"It's from the movie I saw," says StingRay. "*The Fairy Treasure.* You have to be Wiggy. Here, let me explain."

"You guys," Plastic calls out. "StingRay is gonna tell us about the movie!"

Lumphy and the mice trot over to listen. Highlander perks up. Even Sheep rolls over, yawning.

Plastic bounces down to join her friends, and StingRay looks upon them all from the wonderful height of the bed. They are all paying so much attention!

"The movie theater is big," StingRay says. "Bigger than a school, if you've been to school like I have. It's dark inside and smells like popcorn. People eat popcorn in the movies. It's a whole room full of people eating the same food in the dark, just popcorn. Oh, and candy. Then the movie comes on, and it's like being in a cave that's full of butter smell—"

"A cheese cave!" cries Plastic. "Cheese is when you put milk in a cave!"

"I'm telling about the movie," StingRay reminds her.

"Tell the story!" squeaks the mouse called Bonkers. "Tell it now!"

StingRay fluffs her plush out. "Princess DaisySparkle is the kindest, most excellent princess that ever lived," she explains, "and she's so special the whole kingdom loves her. She wears a royal blue dress and then a sky blue dress. She has hair down her back really long, and she rides a unicorn. She has an ugly fairy pet called Wiggy, and these mean guys try to get the fairy treasure."

"Ooh!" cries Bonkers. "Mean guys."

StingRay continues: "DaisySparkle meets a prince, and a witch is chasing after them—all green in the face, with teeth. She lives in an underground lair."

"What's the name of the prince?" asks Lumphy.

"It's not important," says StingRay. "He's a prince. Then DaisySparkle wears a navy blue dress and saves the treasure but she gets caught, and the ugly fairies come to her rescue, and then it's the end. It was so, so good."

"What happens with the witch?" asks Lumphy.

"They get rid of her."

"And what about the prince?" Lumphy wants to know.

"She marries him at the end and that's when she wears this dress that's robin's egg blue with silver trim," answers StingRay.

"Does he get a fairy pet, too?"

StingRay harrumphs. "These other guys are not important, I told you. DaisySparkle is important. I'll explain it while we play, okay? Highlander, you can be my unicorn, and Plastic's going to be Wiggy, and Mice, you can be the ugly fairy friends. Lumphy, you can be the witch if you want."

Lumphy is not sure.

"Do you want to be the prince? You can be the prince."

Lumphy does not answer. He would like to be somebody important.

"Sheep?" StingRay jumps down and pokes the one-eared sheep. "Sheep, you be the witch, okay? Because Lumphy will be the prince."

Sheep does not reply, because she is not awake.

"I'll be the witch," Lumphy finally decides.

"Good. Your name is Cackle." StingRay goes under the bed. Last time she was supposed to clean her room, Honey shoved a bunch of dress-up clothes under there. StingRay attempts to adorn herself in a sky blue handkerchief—but it is too small to stretch around her plush body. She tries again, this time wrapping herself in two necklaces and a small white feather boa.

Not blue enough.

StingRay concocts a new outfit of navy ribbon and a crocheted blue scarf, but discards that as well. Finally she settles on a plastic tiara, accessorized with a lacy royal blue sock from Honey's laundry bin.

All the other toys have been waiting

quite

a

long

time

when StingRay emerges from under the bed and asks: "Do I look like a princess?"

"Aha!" yells Lumphy as Cackle, wearing a black velvet Barbie cape. "You rotten DaisySparkle! I'm going to steal your ugly fairy pet and kidnap her to my witchy lair. Wiggy, I've got you!" He leaps on Plastic and drags her away to the space underneath Highlander.

"Wait!" cries StingRay. "You can't kidnap my fairy!"

"But I already did!" Lumphy laughs his evil laugh and squeezes Plastic in his forepaws.

"Kidnapped! Kidnapped!" yells Plastic.

"And your underground lair can't be Highlander," objects StingRay. "He's my unicorn."

"It's my lair . . . because I'm in it," growls Lumphy. "I've captured your unicorn, too. How 'bout that?"

"I wasn't ready!" cries StingRay. "We didn't even start and now you're kidnapping everybody!"

Plastic bounces forward. "I can escape, right, DaisySparkle? Can't Plumcake escape? Can't she fly?"

"Wiggy," corrects StingRay. "*Wiggy* is your name, and you're a boy."

Plastic stops bouncing. "I don't want to be a boy," she protests. "I'm a girl."

"It's pretend, Plastic," says StingRay. "In pretend, girls can be boys, and boys can be girls. Anyone can be whatever they want. Look: Lumphy is being a witch, right?"

"Yeah, but I'm a boy witch," says Lumphy.

"You are not!"

"I am, too. I'm going to magic your unicorn and turn

it into a dragon for me to ride on!" cries Lumphy, grabbing a pickup stick and using it for a wand. "And I'll magic the ugly fairies, too. Mice, you all have been turned into gremlins, and you must do my evil bidding!"

"Oooh, make me a gremlin!" pleads Plastic. "Make me a girl gremlin! Magic me!"

"Stop!" cries StingRay. "You guys are playing it all wrong."

"It's pretend," Lumphy reminds her. "Anyone can be whatever they want."

"Gremlin! Gremlin!" yells Plastic.

"But it's not the movie!" StingRay bangs her tail on the floor. "And you took my unicorn. That's not what's supposed to happen!"

Lumphy brandishes his wand. Why can't he play the way he wants? "Cackle is turning you into a . . . a . . . a *spoon*, DaisySparkle!" he cries. "Because you are a no-fun bossyboots."

Why is Lumphy ruining everything? StingRay will not have it. "I'm not a spoon, *you're* a spoon!" she cries, grabbing one end of the wand.

"No, *you're* a spoon!" yells Lumphy.

"You!"

"Spoon!"

"Then you're a fork!" cries StingRay.

"Spoon is worse!"

"No, fork is worse!"

"Don't call me fork!" cries Lumphy, dropping the wand and launching himself at StingRay. He bats her face with a buffalo paw and sinks his teeth into her left flipper.

"Oww!" If StingRay could bleed, she would be bleeding a lot right now.

Lumphy chomps harder, and StingRay swings her long tail around and hits him in the head. Wonk!

And again. Wonk!

And finally—Wonk! Lumphy lets go. Oof!

Lumphy has a chunk of StingRay's plush in his teeth. Pthheeh. But while he is spitting out plush, StingRay bangs him upside the head with a flipper. Bap!

Sheep is now awake and bleating in distress, while Plastic bounds around the room squealing, "Stop! Stop!"

The mice—Bonkers, Millie, Brownie, and Rocky— view the proceedings as entertainment. StingRay bangs Lumphy with the other flipper, this time on his woolly buffalo neck. "Ooh," squeaks Millie. "She landed a good one on him, there!"

"They need to control their tempers," says Rocky. "They should use their words."

StingRay hits Lumphy in the tummy with her tail— Bap!—knocking him over.

Now Lumphy, back on his feet, lowers his head and shakes his buffalo horns. He is so angry! StingRay is such a bossyboots all the time!

Charge!

Rumpa lumpa,

Rumpa lumpa,

Lumphy goes for StingRay like a bull in a bullfight.
He rams his horns into her, tearing a hole in her side, then
tosses her up, through the air, and across the room,
where—Fwap!—she lands in the big toy box.

Lumphy doesn't care if StingRay is hurt. He doesn't
care if she never talks to him again.

Horrible, bossyboots StingRay.

Still wearing his cape, Lumphy runs,

Rumpa lumpa,

Rumpa lumpa,

out of Honey's bedroom, past the bathroom—and into
the grown-up bedroom.

. . . . .

Honey's room is silent except for the

thump ump

ump ump

uhhhh of Plastic, letting herself cease bouncing,

and rolling to a stop. "Are you okay, StingRay?" she calls into the quiet.

A flipper peeks over the edge of the big toy box, and waves weakly.

"She's okay!" cry the mice.

"She's the winner!" whispers Bonkers to Millie. "I knew she could win. She's got a great tail, hasn't she? And Lumphy hasn't got any tail at all, just a stumpy bit."

StingRay's flipper grabs hold of the box's edge, and she hauls herself over onto the carpet. Plastic inspects her wound. "You have a hole," she tells StingRay. "You're going to need to get it sewn up if you don't want your stuffing coming out."

StingRay nods. Then her face crumples and her mouth turns down and her eyes squinch—and she would be crying tears if she could, and anyway, she *is* crying, just without the tears.

Frrrrrr, frrrrrr.

There is no Lumphy here to tell her not to panic.

. . . . .

Lumphy has hardly ever been in the grown-up bedroom before. The bed is lower than Honey's but so wide it takes up almost the whole room. The closet is enormous, and through another door is a bathroom inhabited by purple towels whom Lumphy doesn't know very well. Two tall dressers loom at the far end, and in between them is a low wooden chair with a basket on it. There are no toys, and nothing underneath the bed except a momsock and a cookbook.

Lumphy stomps in furious circles under the bed for several minutes. Then he emerges and begins kicking the wooden chair with his left hind leg.

That StingRay! Lumphy kicks again.

She always has to be the important one.

She always wants to make the rules.

"Hitting me with her tail," he mutters to himself. "As if a tail is so useful. As if a tail is such a great thing to have."

Another kick.

"I don't know why Honey took *her* to the movies, any-way," Lumphy grunts. "*I* would have liked to see a movie. *I* would have liked it as much as StingRay. I would have liked it *more*, actually."

Another kick. Harder, this time, and ooohhh, the chair wobbles and—the basket on it tips. The stuff in the basket tumbles out: yarn and thread and needles and fabric. It is a craft basket, and several balls of rainbow yarn land on top of Lumphy. He jerks his head around, but that only serves to stick his horns tight into an acrylic-blend ball. He rolls on his back,

on his side,

on his back,

oofa

oofa

oofa

and around some more, trying to get out from under. Soon, poor Lumphy is tangled in rainbow yarn, and he can't seem to *un*tangle, no matter how he rolls, and without thinking, he cries out, "StingRay, help!"

But no StingRay helps, this time.

And he knows: no StingRay is coming.

StingRay is wounded. Her flipper has a hole in it, made by buffalo teeth and horns.

Lumphy lies on his side, tangled in yarn.

For a long while.

Finally, when he hears the sound of the family car pulling into the driveway, Lumphy struggles to his feet. He takes something from the craft basket in his mouth and shuffles underneath the grown-up bed, his feet jumbled in yarn and his head bowed with the weight of a ball of rainbow acrylic on his horns.

. . . . .

"As soon as Honey sees me, she'll have me mended," StingRay tells Plastic. "She'll be so mad that Lumphy made a hole in me, she'll take care of it right away. Then she'll punish Lumphy really bad."

This idea makes Plastic nervous. "Punish him how?"

"Oh, she'll spank him with dry spaghetti

or maybe make him drink nasty fruit-punch-tasting

medicine.

Or she'll give him sixty-eight time-outs

where he has to sit in a bucket by himself in the hall-

way," says StingRay, as if she knows.

But when Honey comes in, smelling of toothpaste and

strawberry soap, she takes StingRay to bed as usual—

without noticing the hole.

How can Honey not see that there is a gaping hole in

StingRay's flipper, with stuffing peeking out? Exactly

where there was no hole at all when they went to the

movies and had all that specialness together?

Honey goes to sleep after ten pages of the story about

the mouse in the dungeon, but StingRay lies there, awake,

long after eight-thirty, patting her own wounded flipper

in the dark and saying, "There, there, it'll be okay," be-

cause nobody else is around to say it.

. . . . .

It is midnight by the time the grown-ups fall asleep.
The house is dark, and from his hiding place under the
parents' bed, Lumphy can hear the toy mice giggling. It
sounds as if Highlander and Sheep are having a conversa-
tion and Plastic is in the bathroom, bouncing around.
Lumphy can hear her showing off for TukTuk. Still trailing yarn, with a ball of rainbow acrylic on his head, and
holding the something he got from the craft basket between his teeth, Lumphy limps to Honey's room. It is
slow going, as his feet are tangled and his head woefully
heavy, but Lumphy gets there and asks the toy mice to
untangle his legs and pull the ball of yarn off his horns.

Quietly, he climbs onto the high bed, where StingRay
and Honey are sleeping. He taps StingRay's tail, hoping
to wake her up.

She doesn't move.

"Psst. StingRay," whispers Lumphy. "Look what I
brought."

She doesn't wake.

Carefully, Lumphy takes the something in his paws. It is a needle, already threaded with blue thread. Lumphy pokes it into the edge of StingRay's wound with his front feet, then pulls it through the other side with his buffalo teeth. Holding a bit of thread down with one foot, he loops the needle through and pulls it tight to make a knot. Then he sews up StingRay's hole in neat stitches, pushing in with the forefeet and pulling out with the teeth, until it's time to make another knot. He bites the thread so as not to leave any of it trailing, and scurries back to the grown-up bedroom to return his supplies to the craft basket, which Honey's mom has straightened up.

. . . . .

StingRay wakes at five in the morning.

Her flipper feels different. Feels better. She twists her head to look at it and sees a lovely row of royal blue stitches, almost invisible unless you were looking for them. She is fixed. She is good as new!

At first she thinks Honey must have done it, but Honey is sound asleep with her mouth slightly open, and StingRay has to admit that Honey never wakes at night unless she has a nightmare.

StingRay moves to the edge of the bed and peeks over to see if any toys are awake. Nobody is. Sheep is tipped over beneath Highlander and the mice are cuddled together under the toy box where they like to hide.

Lumphy has returned. He's asleep in his favorite spot on the fringed pillow on the floor.

But what's that? StingRay leaps down and scoots over to look more closely. A piece of royal blue thread trails from Lumphy's mouth. It is the same thread as StingRay's stitches.

Now StingRay understands. Lumphy must have done it.

StingRay doesn't know how he managed, but Lumphy must have sewed her up.

With blue.

A beautiful, wonderful color of blue, which is already the best color of all the colors there are in the world.

If that isn't an apology, StingRay decides, it is something awfully close.

Maybe it is even something better.

CHAPTER THREE

⚜

The Garbage-Eating Shark (Which Is Not the Same as the Possible Shark)

One evening, Lumphy, Plastic, StingRay, and Sheep are watching a documentary about beagle dogs on television. Honey and her parents are out at a nighttime party.

During the commercials, Sheep has been telling everyone all about the time she went outdoors and there was actual grass and she chewed it when nobody was looking.

Sheep tells this story a lot. She doesn't seem to remember that everyone has heard it before.

Plastic isn't paying attention. She is wondering why beagle dogs seem familiar, even though she doesn't think she has ever seen a beagle dog.

When the show is over, there comes a documentary called *Great White Sharks: Fearsome Fiends of the Briny Deep.*

"Shark! Shark!" cries Plastic, bouncing vigorously. "I got eaten by a shark once!"

"Oh no," mumbles StingRay. She is afraid of sharks. In particular, she is afraid of the kind that is so big it could eat garbage. Or a plush stingray. And not even notice that it wasn't eating food.

"I mean," says Plastic, correcting herself, "I *nearly* got eaten by a shark."

"You did?" asks Lumphy. Because Plastic has never said a word until now.

"Well, a possible shark. A garbage-eating, ball-eating possible shark. Yes!" cries Plastic. "At the beach one time. I know all about these guys."

She is excited to see what they look like on TV, because the one that carried her around in its mouth at the beach was not anything she got an especially good look at.

StingRay announces she is going upstairs. "It's eight o'clock," she says, over her shoulder. "And since eight-thirty is when I always go to sleep with Honey, I should start getting ready for bed."

"But she's not here. She's at a nighttime party," notes Lumphy.

"I don't want to be off-schedule tomorrow," StingRay demurs.

"Won't you stay and watch the sharks?" asks Plastic, twirling. "The sharks are going to eat stuff with their big big teeth!"

"I wish I could, but it's my bedtime," says StingRay. "You have your fun." She lurches up the steps.

On the television, an enormous fish with teeth charges through the water to eat a piece of meat that is hanging off the back of a boat.

"Hm," says Plastic.

Now another enormous fish swims past the camera, then eats a baby seal.

"Hm," says Plastic again.

"What?" asks Lumphy.

"I don't want to say," says Plastic.

"You can't say 'hm' over and over without saying what you mean."

"It's just . . . it's not the same kind of shark, I guess," says Plastic.

"That ate you?"

"Mine had fur," says Plastic. "And went on four legs. And it was spotty, like the beagle dogs."

"It was furry?" asks Sheep.

"Yes. And it made that same barky noise, like the beagle dogs do."

"Then it wasn't a shark," says Sheep.

"It wasn't?"

"Sharks are fish," explains Sheep. "I thought every-body knew that."

They watch for a few minutes as a scientist explains that sharks *do* eat garbage by mistake sometimes, and that dead sharks have been found with license plates, tires, and hunks of wood inside their stomachs.

"Hm," says Plastic.

"What?" Lumphy wants to know. "What 'hm'?"

"I think I was eaten by a beagle dog, then," says Plastic. "Not a shark."

"Being eaten by a beagle dog is still scary," says Lumphy, comfortingly.

. . . . .

Two days later, Honey comes upstairs after school holding a large package that has arrived in the mail. It is a cardboard box. The return address reads "Grandpa" and then a street name and number.

StingRay is watching from on top of the high bed with

the fluffy pillows. Lumphy and Plastic are watching from a shelf. Honey plonks the box on the carpet beside her bed and kneels down to rip the tape off the outside.

Inside the box is something wrapped in bubble wrap and surrounded by small pieces of Styrofoam. Honey looks at the present but doesn't bother to take it out right away. Instead, she grabs the top piece of bubble wrap and begins popping the bubbles with sharp snaps.

"Honey?" her mom calls up the stairs. "Shay's dad is on the phone. He wants to know if we'd all like to go over there for the afternoon."

Honey drops her bubble wrap, grabs her box of Barbie dolls and clothes, and runs downstairs. "Taking the silent Barbies again," mutters StingRay.

There is a sudden movement on the floor.

The cardboard box is rocking from side to side.

It is actually hopping and jerking across the carpet like a fish out of water. And it is making a noise.

Grunk! Gru-GRUNK!

Grunk! Gru-GRUNK!

The thing that's wrapped in bubble wrap wants to get out.

Plastic and Lumphy leap onto the high bed and cuddle up to StingRay.

Grunk! Gru-GRUNK! goes the cardboard box.

It scoots across the floor, rocking and jerking.

Grunk! Gru-GRUNK!

They can hear Styrofoam peanuts crunching and the bubbles of the bubble wrap popping.

Pippity-pop, gru-GRUNK!

Pippity-pop, gru-GRUNK!

Finally, a voice like a bugle yells from inside the box. "I got my head out. The head is out, people!"

The toys look at one another.

The voice continues: "Anyone here with hands or teeth? Hands or teeth, anyone?"

Lumphy has teeth. But he doesn't mention them. He is not feeling very tough and brave, somehow.

StingRay can do a lot with her flippers; they are almost like hands—but she doesn't mention them, either.

The bugle voice comes again. "The kid left me tied up in here."

Silence.

Plastic is relieved that she doesn't have any hands or teeth like the cardboard box is asking for.

"I don't think they're supposed to do that, are they?" the voice goes on. "They usually take you out and play with you, right?"

The one-eared sheep rolls across the carpet and sniffs the box. "Did you say something about teeth?" she asks, dimly.

"Teeth! Yeah. Anyone with teeth?"

"I don't hear very well," explains Sheep. "It's my ear, you see. I lost it."

"I can't see your missing ear. I can't see jack!" yells the thing in the box.

"I have teeth," Sheep tells it. "Once, I went outside and there was actual grass and I chewed it when Honey wasn't looking. I even got some clover, I think. Actual grass, can you believe it?"

"Fantastic!" yells the thing in the box.

Sheep pokes her nose into the bubble wrap. She begins to chew on the tape that surrounds whatever is inside.

The thing in the box holds still.

Lumphy, StingRay, and Plastic watch from the bed as Sheep chews, rhythmically.

She chews for a long time.

The thing in the box doesn't speak.

When she is done, the one-eared sheep burps. "Tape is sweet," she says to herself. "I wouldn't have thought it."

Sheep is not curious about what is in the box because she has forgotten why she began chewing. Fatigued by her efforts, she rolls away under the bed and is asleep almost before she gets there.

The toy mice are hiding and nowhere to be found. The box is still.

Lumphy is looking for his courage. He whispers to himself, "I am a toughy little buffalo. A toughy buffalo. A toughy. A buffy. A tough-a-buff."

"You're a what?" StingRay asks him.

"A tough-a-buff."

"What does that mean?"

"It means I'm tough and brave. And I'm going down to see what's in the box. Are you coming with me?"

"I was going anyway," StingRay lies. "I was waiting for Sheep to be finished."

But while they've been discussing, up on the high bed, the plump mouse Bonkers has scooted over to the box. "It was nice to Sheep, right?" he calls to Lumphy. "So I'm going to say hello!"

"Okay," calls Lumphy, still on the bed. "You go for it."

Bonkers creeps to the top of the box. "Sheep is finished with your tape, I think! You can come out now."

The cardboard box gives a tremendous whump!

And then

Grunk! Gru-GRUNK!

Grunk! Gru-GRUNK!

Out from the crunching, popping bubble wrap emerges

a large

gray

rubber

hollow

toothy

garbage-eating

fearsome fiend of the briny deep

great

white

shark.

Ahhhhhhhh!

Plastic bounces at top speed out of Honey's room and down the stairs. Lumphy and StingRay leap off the foot of

the bed and follow. Hardly even caring if the people are home (although they are not; they have gone to Shay's), the toys run to the kitchen—

Rumpa lumpa, rumpa lumpa.

Frrrrrr, frrrrrr.

Boing, boing, boing!

Around through the pantry,

eeeeerrrrrrr—

and down another flight of stairs.

Rumpa lumpa, rumpa lumpa.

Fwap! Gobble-a gobble-a.

Fwap! Gobble-a gobble-a.

Boing, boing, boing!

Bonk!

Into the basement, where the shark will not find them.

. . . . .

StingRay has never been in the basement before. Plastic was there once, when Honey's mother repaired her with industrial-strength tape, and Lumphy (who gets dirty a lot) comes down often to visit Frank, the washing machine.

StingRay is almost more scared of the dusty, spidery corners of the basement than she is of the garbage-eating shark.

But not quite. The three toys skitter across the cold floor and leap into a laundry basket filled with dad-clothes. They hide under a pair of pajamas and listen for the Grunk! Gru-GRUNK!

But the basement is quiet.

And still quiet.

Until Frank talks.

"Lumphy!" he cries. "I haven't seen you all week."

"Hi, Frank." Lumphy peeks his head out. Still no shark.

"Don't be shy, little buffalo," says Frank. "I can see your friends under there, and I've guessed your plan."

"You have?" asks Lumphy. Because he has no plan.

"It's a party, right?" Frank says gleefully. "That's why you brought your little pals."

Lumphy is so surprised he doesn't answer.

"My first-ever party," Frank continues. "I can't believe you thought to surprise me. Is there gonna be cake?"

"Rarrrahh," says the Dryer, a dusty brown contraption next to Frank.

"Oh, don't be such a spoilsport," Frank snaps at her. "It is *too* a party. Lumphy, you shouldn't have. A party all for me?"

The Dryer grunts.

"It could be for you, too," concedes Frank. "But I thought you said you didn't think it *was* a party."

"Roorgaah."

"Fine. Don't be logical. Lumphy!" Frank calls. "How do we start? I've never been to a party before."

Lumphy is going to explain that they are escaping from a shark, not arriving at a party at all, when Frank interrupts: "Me and the Dryer—we're both just thrilled."

Lumphy can't bear to tell them the truth. "We were trying to get a real cake," he fibs. "But we could only get an imaginary one. It's right there in front of you. Choco-late peanut-butter mocha vanilla banana flavor, with frosting roses."

Plastic catches on. "It's a party!" she yells, bouncing out of the laundry basket and hopping onto Frank's lid. "Happy party, everybody!"

"That's Plastic," explains Lumphy. "And this is StingRay."

StingRay, still hidden under dad-pajamas, sticks one flipper out and waves.

"Party!" yells Plastic. "Party, party, party!"

"You can come out, StingRay," says Frank. And then, about the Dryer, "I know she's not much to look at, but she doesn't bite."

"Hrmph," says the Dryer, offended.

"A joke, a joke," Frank tells her. "You know I think you're beautiful."

"StingRay is scared of basements," says Lumphy. "Do

you think you could sing her a song, Frank? Because then she wouldn't be scared, and you're such a good singer, it would really add to the party."

"Of course," booms Frank. "And I know there are some towels here who won't want to miss the chance to back me up. Towels, wake up! We're gonna sing!"

A pile of folded purple towels, sitting on top of the dryer, awake from the slumber in which they spend the largest part of every day.

"What's going on?" asks one.

"Frank wants us to sing," explains another.

"Frank is all the time singing," complains a third. "Hey. Is that the ball we see sometimes in the bathroom?"

"Yeah," answers the first. "The Girl's ball."

"I thought I recognized her."

"Just freestyle it with me, okay?" begs Frank. "Sing backup."

"We're always your backup," mutters the second towel. "You never ask if any of us wants to sing lead, do you?"

But Frank isn't listening. Instead, his big beautiful voice is belting out:

"StingRay, wing-ray,

We all stand up and

SING-ray!

StingRay, fling-ray,

What a special

Thing-ray!

Sing it out loud!

Sing it out,

Sting it out!

Singy, Stingy,

Wingy, Thingy,

Stingy, sting,

StingRAY!"

The towels are humming and oooh oooh oohing, and when Frank sings it all over again, some of them do harmonies. It is very impressive.

During the repeat, StingRay comes out from underneath the dad-pajamas and claps her flippers together. Lumphy is dancing, wagging his tail stump and shaking his buffalo body. Plastic is bouncing.

By the third time through, Frank's lights are blinking and he's tilting slightly back and forth. StingRay is tossing her tail around and jumping on the clothes in the laundry basket, while Plastic has added an extra spin to her rhythmic bounce.

"Dance party! Dance party!" Plastic screams.

And it is.

They follow "The StingRay Song" with "Greasy Little Buffalo." Then a number called "Love Train," which Frank and the towels know from the radio. StingRay wraps her flippers around Plastic and they roll together in circles on the dusty basement floor. Frank bangs his lid up and down and the towels shimmy their corners as much as towelly possible. Then StingRay grabs Lumphy's paw and they wiggle and kick and swish their backsides while Plastic bounces so high she hits the basement ceiling.

Finally, everyone collapses in exhaustion; even Plastic.

The music over, they sit around happily chatting and eating slices of the imaginary chocolate peanut-butter mocha vanilla banana cake, with frosting roses for all. StingRay puts her flipper around Plastic and says, "You see? There's nothing to be frightened of in the basement. It may be dark and dusty, but it's perfectly safe."

"I know," says Plastic.

"I mean, it might be scary for the mice," says StingRay, "because they're small and the washer and dryer are so big, but it's not scary for larger toys like you and me."

Oh no.

Suddenly, Plastic remembers.

The mice! Bonkers, Millie, Brownie, and Rocky. "We left them upstairs with the shark," she says, in a small voice.

"What?"

"We left Sheep up there, too."

"Huh?"

"With the shark."

StingRay is aghast. "Oh, they're going to be so mad."

"If they're . . ." Plastic can't quite say what she's thinking.

"If they're what?"

"Um. If they're still alive."

"It's eating them right now!" StingRay cries. "It thinks they're garbage!

We left them there to get eaten

while we had a dance party!

I can't believe it.

We're horrible friends.

Horrible!

I hate myself," moans StingRay. "Lumphy, stop talking to the towels. We have to go! The shark is eating Sheep and the mice!"

Lumphy takes in the situation and feels like he might throw up, even though he doesn't even eat. "What should we do?" he asks.

"Oh, the poor mice!" continues StingRay, ignoring his question. "Shoved into a shark stomach

with bits of cardboard

and sour-milk smell; ·

chewed into tiny bits of mouse mixed with

green beans

and things with mold on them . . .

Ooooh, that's it!" StingRay waves her flipper, inspired. "Garbage. We need garbage."

"How come?" Plastic wants to know.

"It's a garbage-eating shark, right?"

"Right."

"So if we stuff it full of garbage, at least it won't be able to eat anyone *else*," explains StingRay. "Come on!"

. . . . .

There is no time to be secretive. Lumphy, StingRay, and Plastic dash upstairs to the kitchen and open the cabinet under the sink. Lumphy pulls with his teeth and StingRay yanks with her flippers and together they grab the plastic garbage bag and drag it out of its bin. Grunting and huffing, they lug it up the stairs while Plastic bounces at top speed into Honey's bedroom.

There she finds the shark on one corner of the rug, right next to Sheep and Bonkers. It looks as if it's about to eat them! And where are the other mice? Oh dear, oh dearie, it is too late!

Plastic takes a good hard bounce on the floor and launches herself at the shark, hitting it hard on its back. Ooof! "Take that, you mouse-eater!" she yells.

Still waiting for Lumphy and StingRay to get up the stairs with the garbage, she retreats briefly, then bounces the shark again.

"Ouch," the shark says as Plastic readies herself for a third bounce. "Would you back off for a minute, roundie?"

"You big mean mouse-eater!" cries Plastic, and she bounces it again, ooof!—this time knocking the shark off its tummy and onto its side.

"Hey!" it yells. "Mind your manners!"

Sheep and Bonkers rush to safety underneath Highlander, just as StingRay and Lumphy struggle in with the bag of trash.

"Sit on it, Lumphy!" cries StingRay. "Hold it down!"

Lumphy (very bravely) launches himself onto the body of the weakened rubber shark, pinning it to the floor with his forefeet and holding it down with his bottom while StingRay grabs bits of garbage from the bag and shoves them into the shark's hollow insides.

Spluurk! In goes an orange peel.

Splot! A used tissue.

Spluurk! Another orange peel.

The shark is struggling and tossing its head, snapping its jaws, but Plastic gives it a hard bounce on the nose and StingRay keeps shoveling in the garbage.

A wet coffee filter.

Moldy blueberries.

A rubber band.

A half-eaten pancake.

Old tofu.

Soggy lettuce.

An unwanted carrot.

All of it goes into the hollow shark until it can't hold any more and its jaws are wedged open.

"There!" cries StingRay. "Now you can't eat any more mice!"

"Ngggaagaarrrice," says the shark with its mouth full.

"The bedroom is safe!" StingRay calls out to Sheep and

whatever mice have survived. "You can come out now. If we work together we can all tie the shark down with some yarn before Honey gets home from her playdate."

Sheep rolls out slowly from beneath Highlander.

She is followed by Bonkers. And Millie.

And Brownie.

And Rocky.

They are all there. All four mice.

"Oh. Um. Hi," says StingRay.

"I thought you were eaten," says Plastic.

"We saved you!" StingRay announces, standing on her tail and waving her dirty flippers around. "We didn't run away, like maybe it seemed like we did; we didn't run away or go to a dance party. Oh, ha!" She chuckles to herself. "Like we would have a dance party at a time like this, heh heh."

"Excuse me," says Sheep, agitated. "If Lumphy keeps sitting on my new friend, how can we have our chewing club?"

"What new friend?" snaps StingRay.

"What club?" wonders Lumphy.

"While you guys were gone, we invented it," explains Sheep. "Me, the shark, and Bonkers. Remember how I chewed the grass that one time when I went outside? And I chewed a shoelace before, too. And she"—Sheep gestures with her lone ear at the shark—"she only just got here and already she's done cardboard and bubble wrap. So we thought we'd have a club." Sheep looks at the shark, underneath Lumphy, its mouth stuffed with garbage. "But if you keep doing *that* to her, I don't know if it's going to work out."

"I just now did a bit of cardboard!" cries Bonkers. "I did. I chewed it. Do you want to see?" He scurries over to the box and shows them a tiny nibble. "So I can join the club, too!"

"I didn't even know he had teeth," whispers StingRay to Lumphy.

"Yeah, they've all got teeth," says Lumphy, who is still sitting on the shark. "Just tiny mouse ones."

"Oh," says StingRay, who doesn't have any teeth at all.

"Geewi Gugu Gorgareerrica," says the shark.

"Oh, right!" cries Bonkers. "It's gonna be called the Chewing Society of North America. Great name, huh?"

Lumphy wants clarification. "You mean, the two of you are in a chewing club with. Um. Her?" He points with his nose to the shark underneath his bottom.

Sheep nods.

"It was the shark's idea," explains Bonkers. " 'Cause sharks are naturally good at chewing. We're gonna make a list of all the stuff we want to chew, too. It's called the List of Chewables. Great name, huh? We're going to start with a sock. Because nobody will notice if a sock is missing. People lose socks all the time, right?"

"Oh no," says Plastic. "I think we made a mistake."

"Don't be hasty," says StingRay. "Let me get this clear. Sheep, did this shark attempt to eat you?"

Sheep shakes her head.

"Did it try to eat the mice?"

Sheep shakes her head again.

"It was only chewing, not eating?"

Sheep nods.

"Everyone up here was fine, all this time, and you were just sitting around forming clubs together and not even wondering what happened to us?"

"Yes," answers Sheep.

StingRay glares at Plastic. "You *told* me she was eating everybody! You told me they probably *weren't even still alive.*"

"Oops!" says Plastic, bouncing lightly. She rolls over to the shark. "Hello. My name is Plastic. And I'm not a roundie, I'm a ball. I'm made of rubber, like you."

The shark doesn't reply.

"And um. I am sorry I bounced you," Plastic continues. "I am sorry I bounced you a lot of times, actually."

Nothing from the shark.

"I just. I got almost eaten one time by a beagle dog and I got really, really scared when you started with that Gru-GRUNK that you do. You know how you go?"

The shark nods, a very tiny nod.

"I think I don't understand chewing," Plastic goes on. "Because I don't have a mouth, or any teeth. Because of being a ball. That's normal for a ball, not to have those things. I can smell, though," she adds. "And see and hear. Even though I don't know how I do them!"

She is expecting the shark to express interest, because really, what she just said is very interesting, but the shark only twitches. She seems quite weak, now that Plastic looks at her, as if maybe she is choking on all that garbage.

The shark disgorges a small bit of soggy lettuce from her mouth.

"Um. Lumphy?" says Plastic. "I think you should stop sitting on our new friend."

"Oh." Lumphy had forgotten where he was. He climbs off the shark. "We should probably take the garbage out of her," he says, thoughtfully.

"Fine," says StingRay. She rears up on her tail, grabs the shark with her flippers, and begins shaking it over the plastic garbage bag.

Unwanted carrot.

Soggy lettuce.

Old tofu.

Pancake.

Rubber band.

Blueberries.

Coffee filter.

Orange peel.

Used tissue.

More orange peel.

When the shark is empty, StingRay drags her down the hall to the bathroom, while Lumphy shoves the trash bag under Honey's bed. Then together they turn on the bath, put in a plug, and run some water.

The limp, exhausted shark doesn't say a word.

When the water is deep, they add some bubble bath and put her in. The soapy water runs into the shark's hollow cavity and washes out all the leftover bits of garbage.

The shark revives. She begins to swim the length of the bathtub, swishing her thick tail with only her top fin sticking out into the air. It is exactly the way the sharks swam on *Fearsome Fiends of the Briny Deep*—but Lumphy doesn't tell that to StingRay, even though it sends a shiver across his back.

When the shark is clean, they drain the water and dry her off in TukTuk's warm folds.

"I'm really really *really* sorry," says Plastic again, rolling to meet them as they reenter Honey's bedroom.

The shark coughs once and then asks, "You a floater?"

"Why, yes, I am!" says Plastic, pleased.

"All right then," the shark says, gruffly. "Any floater is a friend of mine."

"I'm sorry, too," says Lumphy. "It was a bad mistake."

"What are you, bison or buffalo?" asks the shark.

"Buffalo," Lumphy answers.

"What's the difference?"

Lumphy shrugs. He doesn't actually know. He has never heard of a bison.

"Ha! Just kidding you. There's no difference. Bison, buffalo. It's the same thing!" The shark laughs and turns its eyes to StingRay. "Yes?"

StingRay looks away. "I um . . ."

"What? Cat got your tongue?"

StingRay squirms. "I like the way you swim," she finally says.

"Yah, well. It comes natural when you're a fish," says the shark.

StingRay is mortified. *She* is a fish. But swimming doesn't come naturally to her, because she's made of plush, not rubber.

"Are you gonna say sorry?" asks the shark. "Or not? Because I think I am owed an apology here, and to be honest, I've had a rotten day."

The word sticks in StingRay's throat, but she chokes it out. "Sorry."

And once it has been said, she is surprised to find that she feels a whole lot better. Like she has been holding her breath—if she had breath—and has now, after a long time, exhaled.

"Apology accepted," says the shark. "Now, can anyone recommend a piece of wood or an old bit of junk no one cares about in this place? Because I could really use something to chew."

CHAPTER FOUR

❧

Concerning That Plump Mouse Bonkers, the Vacuum Cleaner, and a Friendship Between Fish

Honey's parents are on a cleaning spree. They are taking it very seriously. StingRay and Lumphy are in Honey's armchair, watching the people as they bustle from room to room. Plastic has been shoved into the toy box.

The adults wipe mildew from the ceiling of the bathroom and pull the books off the shelves to get the dust in the back. The mom takes bag after bag of outgrown clothes to a charity shop, and the dad finds the leftover sack of garbage under the high bed.

"Honey?" the dad calls.

"What?" Honey is downstairs in the kitchen.

"Why do you have garbage under your bed?"

"I don't."

"Yes, you do."

"Oh. I thought I smelled something," says Honey, coming into the room.

Honey knows her toys play when she's not around. After all, they are never exactly where she left them when she returns from school, and last week when she got home from Shay's, the garbage-eating shark was lounging on the carpet with the bubble wrap packaging chewed to bits. But her toys have never done anything like hide trash under the bed.

Lumphy examines her face. Honey is wondering.

"Sorry," she tells her dad as he holds out the bag.

"But why is it in here?" he persists.

She shrugs.

"I can't believe we left the garbage there," whispers Lumphy to StingRay. "It's been a lot of days!"

"I thought you took care of it," StingRay whispers back.

"I thought *you* took care of it," says Lumphy.

The dad clucks his tongue. "There's a ton of junk under here. Will you go get the vacuum cleaner?"

Honey bends and looks under the bed. Several necklaces, crumpled strings of toilet paper, some sky blue ribbon, a plastic tiara, some white lace, and a lacy royal blue sock—StingRay's stash of DaisySparkle costumes is down there. She pulls everything out and spreads it over the patchwork quilt.

Honey sorts through the sparkly things for a minute. Then she picks up—not StingRay, but the shark. The new shark she didn't even look at when it first arrived; the new shark she's hardly even played with. Honey takes that shark and wraps her in lace and sky blue ribbon.

StingRay's lace and sky blue ribbon.

Honey winds a silver necklace four times around the bit of the shark that is most like a neck.

StingRay's silver necklace.

Honey announces, "Dad, I thought of a name for my shark."

"How nice." The dad is pulling bits of LEGO, scraps of paper, and several books out from under the bed.

"Don't you want to hear what it is?"

"Sure. But I asked you to go get the vacuum."

"Her name is DaisySparkle."

StingRay's favorite name. From *StingRay's* favorite movie.

"Great." The dad pulls his head out from under the bed and examines the DaisySparkle shark in her finery. "She looks fancy, doesn't she?"

"She's going to a fiesta," says Honey.

"Can it be a vacuuming fiesta?" asks the dad.

"Okay," Honey agrees. She runs down the hall with the shark, trailing a pretty piece of sky blue ribbon.

StingRay, immobile on the easy chair, cries without tears.

. . . . .

Rrooooooooooooma rooma.

The vacuum makes a very, very large noise.

Rrooooooooooooma rooma.

Lumphy huddles closer to StingRay and puts his buffalo paws over his eyes.

Rrooooooooooooma rooma.

"Tell me when it's over," he says.

"What, are you scared you'll be sucked into the
vacuum cleaner?" StingRay is cranky, watching Honey
do her chores with DaisySparkle shark tucked under
one arm.

"Stranger things have happened," says Lumphy.

"You're way too big to get sucked into the vacuum,"
snaps StingRay. "Get over it. Haven't you seen the people
vacuum, like, a million times?"

Lumphy does not answer. His eyes are squeezed shut.

"Well, haven't you?" presses StingRay.

"Mrwwfflfe mide," Lumphy mumbles into his paws.

"What? You can speak up. They won't hear you with all that noise."

"I always hide."

"I thought you were tough and brave." StingRay is in no mood for this. "Don't fall apart on me now."

The dad is making Honey do a very thorough vacuuming job. She cleans under the bed. He pulls the shoes out of the closet and has her get the corners. He moves the toy box and she vacuums the dust underneath.

And.

A mouse.

She vacuums a mouse.

A toy mouse that was underneath.

Bonkers has been sucked up into the vacuum cleaner with no more sound than a slight bumple wumple.

Lumphy and StingRay see it all from their place on the easy chair. But they cannot move. They cannot call out. Bonkers is somewhere deep inside that loud machine.

"She didn't even notice," whispers StingRay, shocked.

Rrooooooooooooooma rooma.

Finally, Honey switches off the vacuum. Her dad puts it back in the hall closet. Honey grabs the box of silent Barbies and—still holding DaisySparkle—trots downstairs.

Like nothing bad has even happened.

. . . . .

In the middle of the night, when the people have finally all gone to bed, StingRay, Lumphy, Plastic, and the remaining toy mice launch a rescue operation, down the hall to the vacuum cleaner closet.

"Hold up!" yells DaisySparkle, launching herself after them.

"Oh, you needn't trouble yourself," says StingRay. She is still mad about the princess costumes and the attention from Honey.

"Excuse me, but members of the Chewing Society of North America look out for their own," answers DaisySparkle.

"We'll manage without your help." StingRay is polite, but barely. "We got along before you came here, after all."

DaisySparkle ignores her and thumps along after them. Lumphy and StingRay pry open the closet door and drag the vacuum out. There is a small plastic door in its side. Lumphy unlatches it, and—thank goodness— inside is a puffy gray vacuum bag.

Only, it doesn't have a hole at the top. It has, in fact, no discernible opening at all.

"Take that bag thing out," urges Plastic.

Lumphy leans over, grabbing the bag in his paws. He joggles it side to side, and finally pulls it out of the vacuum cleaner and into the hall. The bag is larger than he is, and the hole where it connects to the hose is a tiny round aperture, not much bigger than Bonkers. Lumphy calls down. "Can you hear me?"

There is a very quiet squeaking.

"Alive!" cries Rocky.

"We're here to help you!" calls Lumphy. "Can you see the hole at the back? Climb up to it."

The squeaking becomes muffled. As if Bonkers has his mouth full of dust.

"Can you move yourself at all?"

There is a slight wiggle in a bottom corner of the bag.

"He should never have been under the toy box during vacuuming," says Brownie to her fellow mice. "He should have hid in the bookcase with the rest of us."

"Is he climbing out?" wonders Millie. "Can he do it?"

"He's got dirt on top of him," says Lumphy. "I don't think he can get to the opening."

"Let me shake it." StingRay holds out a flipper. "Maybe he'll fall out."

Lumphy isn't sure. "Won't we get dust all over the hall? How will we clean it up?"

StingRay gives him a serious look. "If we don't get Bonkers out, you know where he's gonna end up, don't you?"

No.

"In the dump, that's where!" cries StingRay. "He'll be tossed in a pile of old sour-milk cartons

and no one will love him anymore

and it will smell like throw-up."

Lumphy hands StingRay the vacuum cleaner bag. She turns it so the hole is pointing at the floor and shakes as hard as she can.

Nothing comes out.

StingRay rears onto her tail and jumps up and down.

More nothing comes out.

"You're doing some good bouncing," says Plastic, kindly.

"But he's still in there," says Lumphy.

"I know." StingRay drops the bag, dispirited.

There is a silence. Then DaisySparkle announces, "I'm gonna try."

"You?" StingRay shakes her head.

"Yeah, me," says DaisySparkle. She hurls herself onto the vacuum cleaner bag. Grunk! Gru-GRUNK!

She chews the part of the bag where they can see Bonkers wiggling.

Grunk! Gru-GRUNK!

She spits out dust and baby powder.

Grunk! Gru-GRUNK!

She chews some more.

Spits.

And now there is a nice-sized hole for Bonkers. "Show yourself, mousie!" calls the shark.

First pink dusty nose, then plump, dirty white mouse, then long softy tail emerges from the vacuum bag. Bonkers shakes himself, scattering dust—and smiles. "The Chewing Society of North America!" he yells,

jubilant, hugging the shark as best he can without any visible arms or legs. "The Chewing Society of North America performed a heroic rescue!"

DaisySparkle pats him with a fin.

Bonkers shakes himself again and runs over to Millie, Brownie, and Rocky. "Hey, did you guys know I was chewing from the inside, too?" he tells them, thrilled. "I was! I chewed the inside and the shark chewed the outside and together we did teamwork!"

"Hooray!" yell the mice.

"You guys should try it," says Bonkers. "I bet you could chew as well as me if you practiced. I chewed myself out of that bag, almost. I really almost did!"

StingRay and Lumphy try to pick up clumps of dirt and chewed vacuum cleaner bag off the hall floor, but it is impossible. "Thanks a lot for the *mess*," StingRay huffs at DaisySparkle.

Eventually, Lumphy trots down to the kitchen and

brings up the whisk broom and a dustpan. They clean as best they can, then shove the vacuum bag back into the machine and hope the people don't notice the hole.

. . . . .

In the morning, when Honey and her family are getting ready for school and work, the mother calls down the stairs, "You know what? I think we've got a mouse living in the hall closet!"

"Really?" Honey and her dad come to see.

The mom is holding the chewed-up vacuum cleaner bag. "There are shreds of it all over," she says.

"Hm," says the dad. "Well, if we see any more evidence, we'll have to trap it and put it outside."

"It chewed a big hole," says Honey. "That was a hungry mouse."

As soon as the people are gone for the day, Bonkers runs to the center of the bedroom and wiggles all around. "Did you hear, did you hear?" he cries. "They said it was a *mouse* that chewed the big hole. They said it was a mouse, and they thought it was a mouse, and it was!" He hops up and down in glee. "It *was* a mouse. It was me! It was me!"

．．．．．

A week or so later, while StingRay and Lumphy are playing Uncle Wiggily, DaisySparkle scoots herself over and nudges StingRay with her nose. "Hey," she says.

"Hello there," StingRay says, drawing a card and moving her Uncle Wiggily rabbit four spaces, as if she's awfully busy.

"Did I tell you I've been chewing the Barbies?" DaisySparkle asks, casually.

"No!" StingRay is so surprised she turns to face the shark.

"Oh, yeah," says DaisySparkle. "You know how Honey keeps putting me in stupid outfits and making me play with those dumb things? Well, as soon as she goes out of the room, I go to town. At first I just did a few small nibbles, but a couple days ago I chewed the leg of one of them. I made some serious dents in it, too."

"You shouldn't do that," says StingRay.

"I didn't break them. I just chewed one on its left leg." The shark coughs. "And."

"And what?"

"Yesterday I got the arm of the other one. I nearly bit off its hand."

"What if they can feel it?" wonders Lumphy from the other side of the Uncle Wiggily board.

"Nah. They never talk. It's no different from chewing a table leg."

"They might talk amongst themselves," Lumphy says. "Like when they're alone in the Barbie box. We don't know for sure, just 'cause we've never heard them."

DaisySparkle shrugs her top fin. "If you're worried about it, I'll stop. But really, if you hung out with those

Barbies as much as I have, you'd know they don't feel the smallest bite. And let me tell you, chewing them is very satisfying."

StingRay is secretly pleased. She doesn't want anyone hurt, but really, she hates those Barbies, too. "You don't like playing dress-up with them?" she asks.

The shark shakes her head. "Hardly. It's like playing with a table leg."

"But you're Princess DaisySparkle," says StingRay. "Honey puts you in all those special blue outfits."

The shark snorts. "I don't want to wear clothes. I like to go natural."

"You do?"

"And if you like my name, take it," says the shark. "Blech."

StingRay can't believe what she is hearing. "You don't want to be DaisySparkle?"

"Can't stand it," says the shark. "Call me Spark, if you don't mind."

"Okay," says StingRay, absorbing the new information. "Spark, would you like to play Uncle Wiggily with us?"

"You betcha!" says Spark, looking at the board game. "Hand me a rabbit, bison! I'm gonna wiggle my Wiggily!"

Maybe it's because DaisySparkle changed her name, or maybe it's because she chewed the silent Barbies—but from that day on, she and StingRay are friends.

CHAPTER FIVE

❧

In Which There Is a Sleepover
and Somebody Needs Repair

When Lumphy wants to visit Frank and have a dance in his washtub, he gets himself sticky with jam. Or soy sauce, or peanut butter. Then Honey puts him in the washer and hangs him up to dry. Of course, Lumphy can go down to the basement for a visit any night he wants, or any day when the people are at work and school. But he enjoys most when he and Frank are together singing their buffalo shuffle song during the wash cycle.

Lumphy doesn't much like talking to the Dryer. In fact, he finds her disagreeable. He can never understand a word she says—it's all rumbling and grunting. And when she's silent, it's even worse. The way she sits there, it always seems as if she's thinking something bad.

Lumphy has never been inside the Dryer. Honey's dad says it has been "on the fritz for ages" and they shouldn't put anything big in, like sneakers or a stuffed buffalo, because then the barrel would get out of line.

So one weekend morning, when Honey takes him downstairs to breakfast, Lumphy (very cleverly, and in the mood to visit Frank) falls into the maple syrup pooled on her plate.

The dad wipes Lumphy off with a dishrag and takes him downstairs. Says hello to the workman in the basement and opens Frank's lid.

Wait! Lumphy wants to yell. Why is there a workman down here?

The Dryer is pulled out from the wall. Tubes and

wires are coming from her back. The workman is doing something to her, but before Lumphy can see more, the dad pops him into Frank's tub and adds soap. Then he shuts the lid and starts the wash cycle.

Warm water gushes in.

"Frank!" whispers Lumphy.

There is no answer.

"Frank, can you hear me?"

Frank gives a grunt that is almost indistinguishable from a regular washing machine noise. He doesn't want the workman to hear him talk.

"What's wrong with the Dryer?" whispers Lumphy, his own voice masked by the sound of the water.

Frank doesn't answer.

"Is she going to be okay?" Lumphy is being swished back and forth in Frank's washtub, but instead of feeling dance-y he is sick to his stomach. How could he have thought mean things about the Dryer? How could he have wished she weren't around, when now she has wires coming out of her?

Again, Frank doesn't answer. He can't, because the workman will hear him.

. . . . .

When the wash cycle is finished and Frank's buzzer goes off, nobody comes to get Lumphy. He sits in Frank's tub, listening to the clank of tools and the music from the radio.

Finally, the man calls up the stairs and Honey's dad comes down. "I don't know if I can fix it," the workman tells him. "You got an old machine. I'm gonna send away for a part, should come in by Wednesday, and I'm hoping that'll give you another couple years with this one. But I'm not gonna promise."

"All right," says the dad.

"If this one's finished, and you buy your new machine from us, the installation's free."

"That would be great."

The two men leave without taking Lumphy out of the washer.

When they are gone, the buffalo pokes his head out from under Frank's lid and looks at the big brown wreck of a dryer. She sits at a sad and awkward angle, pulled out from the wall.

"What's wrong with her?" he asks again.

"She started squeaking," explains Frank, in a voice that has none of its usual energy. "Then her tumble didn't sound right, and yesterday she couldn't dry a load of dad-clothes. Just couldn't get them dry at all. They were damp, I tell you," he sobs. "She had damp dad-clothes in her!"

"I am so sorry," Lumphy tells him.

"Well, yeah," says Frank. "I know."

"I hope you feel better," Lumphy calls to the Dryer.

"She can't answer you," says Frank. "She hasn't even grunted since two days ago."

"Oh."

Lumphy doesn't know what to say. He wishes he could do something to help, but there isn't anything to do.

"Did you hear what they said?" worries Frank. "If they can't fix her, they'll replace her. Like she was nobody. Like she was a used-up piece of trash."

Lumphy nods. He heard, but it is too horrible to think about.

"They'll bring some stranger here to live with me and dry the clothes, expecting me to like it," says Frank. "Don't they see we have feelings?"

"I don't think they do," says Lumphy. "They're nice people, but they really only care about other people, you know?"

"I know," says Frank. "That's how this life is."

. . . . .

Lumphy hangs on a clothesline in the bright spring air of the backyard, where he watches Honey and her mother plant petunias. When he is dry, Honey takes him down and brings him indoors. "We're going on a sleepover," she tells him.

She shoves Lumphy in her backpack along with Plastic, StingRay, a box of glitter makeup, clean clothes, a toothbrush, and a pair of pajamas. Quite a tight fit indeed. Lumphy's hind end is squashed to one side and the toothbrush is poking him in the stomach, while StingRay's left flipper is twisted behind her back and her nose is jammed up against a button.

"Sleepover! Sleepover!" whispers Plastic, joyfully, when the zipper is shut.

"What is it, anyhow?" Lumphy wants to know.

Plastic has no idea.

"A sleepover is when you build a loft," says StingRay. "It's way high in the air, up in a tree,

> like a loft bed in a treetop,
>
> with a tent.
>
> You have blankets up there,

and there are birds that fly over to you with baskets of cupcakes in their beaks.

You eat cupcakes and look down *over* the forest, to the town below.

Then you make wishes on the stars you see, because there are so many stars when you're up on top of the world,

and then you go to sleep.

You are up high, *over* the rest of everything, and you're *sleeping*, so it's a sleepover."

"Hooray!" says Plastic. "I can't wait."

"I wish we didn't have to go in this backpack," complains Lumphy. "It's too small, too dark, and it smells like permanent marker."

Just then, Honey unzips the backpack and takes StingRay out. "I forgot, you don't like the backpack, do you?" she says, giving StingRay a kiss where StingRay's cheeks would be if she had cheeks. "I'll carry you in my arms."

Specialness! Specialness forever and ever! StingRay can't help smiling as Honey zips the backpack closed.

Lumphy and Plastic are in the dark. "How come she remembers that StingRay doesn't like the backpack, but she doesn't remember that *I* don't like the backpack?" mutters Lumphy.

Plastic doesn't know. She doesn't like the backpack, either.

. . . . .

The sleepover is not like StingRay said it would be. It is at Honey's friend Shay's house, in Shay's bedroom. Shay's bedroom is not *over* anything. Actually, it is on the ground floor.

Honey is sleeping over*night* at Shay's.

"Now I get it. This is the indoor over*night* kind of sleepover," says StingRay while the girls are in the kitchen eating dinner. "You know, she didn't say it was *that* kind. If she'd said it was *that* kind, I would have explained it to you."

"That's okay," says Plastic. But she is disappointed.

The toys are sitting on a blow-up mattress on Shay's floor. When the girls finish eating, they come in and play Clue until Shay discovers it was Colonel Mustard in the conservatory with the lead pipe. Then they put glitter makeup on each other. Shay also puts glitter makeup on her stuffed duck while Honey tries on dress-up clothes.

StingRay would really like some glitter makeup.

Plastic would really like some glitter makeup, too.

Even Lumphy would not mind some glitter makeup, so long as he could wash it off, later.

But Honey isn't playing with them, checking on them, or even talking about them. She is *pulling her Barbie box* out of a plastic shopping bag. She brought that stupid box and those silent Barbies along on the sleepover!

Honey and Shay dress the Barbies,

and undress the Barbies,

and brush their hair,

and put their hair in ponytails,

and dress the Barbies,

and undress the Barbies,

and wonder why one of them has teeth marks

on its leg,

and why the other one has teeth marks on its

hand,

and then forget about that

and dress the Barbies,

and undress the Barbies,

and brush their hair,

and dress the Barbies again.

For a very long time.

Finally, they pack up and it seems as if maybe they're going to do something with Lumphy, StingRay, and Plastic—but instead, they jump on the blow-up bed and perform a circus extravaganza for Shay's mom, complete with capes, a clown wig, tumbling, and faux-tightrope walking.

Plastic likes the circus, because it's very bouncy. She

wishes she could perform in it—but she isn't invited. Lumphy and StingRay can't even see it. They have fallen off the bed, what with all the jumping, and are lying on the floor—upside down in a pile of dress-up clothes—and missing the entire extravaganza.

Frankly, the whole sleepover is pretty boring and sometimes upsetting.

The girls put on nightgowns and wash themselves in the bathroom, then come back and lie in bed with the lights out, whispering. Whispering so much, StingRay doesn't even get much of a cuddle.

It is very late indeed before their talk dwindles. Sting-Ray, used to going to bed with Honey every night at eight-thirty, sulks herself to sleep long before Lumphy and Plastic deem the house quiet enough to begin moving around.

"Did you see that upside-down spinny thing they did in the circus extravaganza?" asks Plastic, giving a bounce. "I wonder if I could do that."

"I couldn't see," sighs Lumphy. "I was underneath a cape."

"I saw it," pipes up Shay's duck with the glitter makeup. "It's called a handstand forward roll."

"Then I would probably need hands for it, huh?" Plastic rolls over to the duck.

"Probably."

"How do you do?" says Plastic. "I'm a ball."

"I can tell," says the duck. "My name is Buttermilk."

Introductions are made, and Buttermilk explains that all the other toys who talk are in the basement playroom, not the ground-floor bedroom. Shay sleeps with Buttermilk, so the duck almost never gets to talk to anybody unless she navigates the stairs, which is hard to do without legs or sizable flippers. But Shay is kind to her. It is not a bad life, even though Buttermilk is lonely.

"You look excellent with all that makeup on," says Plastic. "I wish I had some. I could be a glitter ball!"

"I think they're going to have to wash me," says the duck, nervously.

"Don't be scared," says Lumphy. "I've been in a washing machine lots of times, and it's not bad at all. In fact, it's—" He breaks off, thinking of Frank and the Dryer.

"What?" asks Buttermilk.

"I have a friend," says Lumphy. "She's having repairs. I don't know if she'll get better."

"Who's having repairs?" asks Plastic.

"The Dryer."

"Oh dearie," says Plastic, and falls silent.

"She was all pulled from the wall with wires showing," Lumphy continues. "Frank is really upset."

"Isn't there something you can do?" asks Buttermilk.

Lumphy shakes his head. "I don't think so. I tried to think of a get-well present, but it's hard to find a present for a dryer. She doesn't play games or wear clothes or eat or read. She can't even talk right now."

"Oh." Buttermilk is on Shay's bed, and she waddles around Shay's sleeping body to the windowsill. "Look outside," she says.

Plastic and Lumphy join her.

"You can wish on a star," says Buttermilk as they gaze at the sky. "That's what I do when there's nothing else."

"That's what StingRay said you could do at sleepovers!" cries Plastic. "Make wishes on stars!"

"Sometimes my wishes come true," offers Buttermilk.

"What do you wish for?" Lumphy asks.

"One time I wished for visitors," says the duck. "And now you're here."

"We're here! We're here!" Plastic spins herself in a circle.

"I also wished for new books, and Shay got a library card."

"Ooh!" Plastic likes that idea.

"And I wished for Shay to stop snoring."

"So let's wish," says Plastic. "We'll pick three different stars and all wish for the Dryer to get better."

"But she might not, anyway," Lumphy worries.

"They don't always come true," concedes Buttermilk as Shay rolls over in her sleep and begins to snore.

"Yes, but then we know we *tried* to get her better," says Plastic. "Then at least we *did* something."

So Lumphy picks a star to the right, and Buttermilk picks a star to the left, and Plastic picks one high up near the moon. And they all wish.

. . . . .

"A sleepover is fun for kids," announces StingRay to Spark and Sheep when Honey brings them home. "However, it is not fun for buffaloes and stingrays and balls, because all they get to do is

lie on the floor lonely and bored,

and not even get played with because people are playing with Barbies, and makeup,

and Barbies,

and clown wigs,

and Barbies,

and board games.

Then everybody goes to sleep on a bed that

isn't even high—

or *over* anything.

And that's all there is to it. It's not even

special."

"Plus you have to go in the backpack to get to it," adds Lumphy. "And there's a new weird smell in there."

"I made a friend!" cries Plastic. "Her name is Buttermilk. We wished on stars!"

"Was there grass?" wonders Sheep, hopefully. "Or maybe clover?"

Plastic shakes her head. Or rather, she shakes her whole self. "There were handstand forward rolls," she says. But neither Spark nor Sheep is particularly interested.

. . . . .

On Wednesday afternoon, Honey and Lumphy are watching television in the living room when the workman comes again for the Dryer. He goes down to the basement with a toolbox and a new part.

Lumphy is thinking so much about Frank and the Dryer, he cannot concentrate on the TV. The show is about some kids who drink pink milk, and Lumphy does not wonder why the milk is pink, or how it got pink, or why they like it pink—the way he would ordinarily. He is strategizing how he can get to the basement without waiting until everyone in the house has gone to sleep.

What can he do?

There is nothing sticky nearby that he can get on his fur.

And he cannot move in front of Honey.

Luckily, Honey decides she wants to make pink milk. She turns off the TV and brings Lumphy to the kitchen. Her mother is in the basement, watching the workman, and her father is not home from work yet. Honey opens the fridge. And the freezer. And two cupboards.

Strawberries. Vanilla ice cream. Milk.

Frozen raspberries.

Then plain yogurt.

Flour.

Ketchup.

Half a tomato.

A jar of pimientos.

Chili sauce.

And barbecue sauce.

Honey puts all these ingredients on the table and begins mixing them in a bowl. She mashes up the strawberries with her fingers and scoops in most of the ice cream from the carton. Then she adds milk and a big squirt of ketchup. Some of the ketchup gets on the table.

A chance! As Honey searches for a whisk, Lumphy tips himself into the puddle of condiment.

"Not again," Honey scolds when she sees him. "You are the messiest buffalo."

But—she doesn't bring Lumphy to the basement. Instead, she wets a dishrag and wipes the ketchup from his body. "You didn't get any in your woolly front fur," she tells him. "So I think we can just wipe it off."

That was not supposed to happen. Lumphy needs to get to the basement as soon as possible. An operation is going on down there!

Honey picks up the half tomato and squeezes the juice into her bowl. Then chili sauce and a few shakes of barbecue. She adds some yogurt and a handful of flour. Her experiment is only a light pink color. She whisks and whisks.

Now she adds frozen raspberries. These make the milky mixture quite a bit pinker, but now it is lumpy. She adds pimientos. Now it is *very* lumpy.

"I need a sieve," Honey says to herself, and rummages for one in a low cupboard. She finds it, gets a large mug, and begins to strain the pink milk.

Lumphy sees his opportunity. The sieve is an inch away from his nose, and Honey is holding it with one hand and pouring with the other—but she is not holding the mug. He takes a risk, while she is concentrating, and—

Bonk!

Lumphy bangs his nose into the sieve and tips the mug over. The pink milk spills across the table, under Lumphy's buffalo belly, and over the edge to the floor. Honey drops the sieve and knocks Lumphy into the puddle of milk. She runs for the dishrag and some paper towels. "Mom!"

Lumphy lies there, triumphant, letting the pink disgustingness soak into his fur.

Any minute now he'll be in the basement.

. . . . .

When Lumphy arrives, the Dryer is still pulled out from the wall, her front door completely off. The workman has a collection of tools spread across the floor, but he is sitting on a plastic lawn chair with a tired expression on his face.

It doesn't look good.

Honey's mother shoves Lumphy into Frank's washtub and grabs TukTuk and some Girl-clothes out of the full laundry basket. She loads the washer and goes back upstairs to deal with the pink milk problem.

The cycle begins. When the water rushes in, Lumphy can no longer hear what's going on in the basement. And he can't talk to Frank, because Frank won't answer with the repairman in the room.

"Hi," Lumphy whispers to TukTuk. "Do you know what's happening with the Dryer?"

"Why would I know?" says TukTuk.

"You were in the laundry basket. Maybe you heard something."

"I don't hear about anything that goes on in this house," fusses TukTuk. "Not that you would care."

"I care," says Lumphy, surprised. He has never known TukTuk to be anything but kind and calm.

"If you do, you don't show it," snaps TukTuk. "I'm

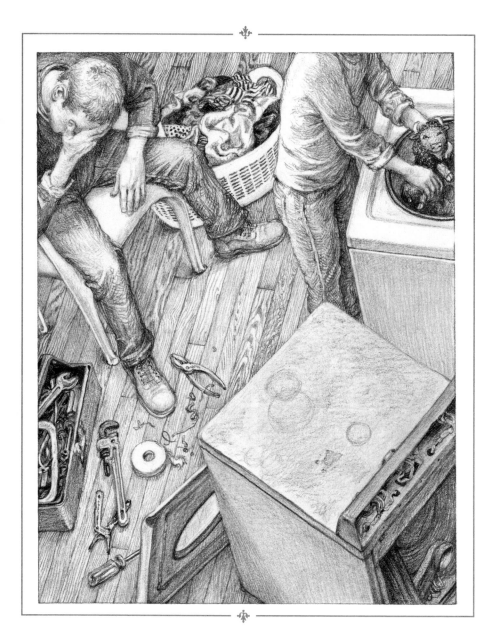

never in the linen closet with the other towels, I'm never in the grown-up bathroom with the *other* other towels. It's rare that I even get *washed* with anybody," she complains. "And even my so-called friends don't tell me what's happening."

"Are you upset I didn't tell you that the Dryer was broken?"

"It's not about the Dryer," sulks TukTuk.

"What's it about, then?" Lumphy asks. The water drains and Frank's tub begins to spin.

"I heard you had a dance party," TukTuk says. "Every other towel in the house was there. They're all talking about it."

"Oh."

"Just because I get washed with the Girl-clothes doesn't mean I don't want to go to a party," says TukTuk.

"I'm—"

"And just because I can't dance doesn't mean I don't want to, either."

Lumphy doesn't know what to say. He wants to make TukTuk feel better, but they are inside Frank's washtub—and he can't say in front of Frank that he had never intended to have that dance party in the first place. So he stays silent, and TukTuk stays silent, too. They let Frank go through his cycle.

When it is done, Frank's buzzer beeps and Honey's mother returns to the basement. She dumps Lumphy and the towels into the hamper while she talks to the workman, who is finally, finally finished. He is putting away his tools, and the Dryer is pushed back against the wall.

"Thanks so much," the mom tells him. "Come up and I'll write you a check." She sets down the laundry basket.

"Don'tcha want to put that in?" he says, gesturing at the damp wash.

"Silly me." She holds up Lumphy. "This can go in as well?"

"Should be okay."

Honey's mother shoves Lumphy and all the towels into the Dryer and turns it on.

The Dryer purrs.

. . . . .

Fwuuumpa! (baggle baggle)

Fwuuumpa! (baggle baggle)

It is seriously hot in the Dryer.

Fwuuumpa! (baggle baggle)

Fwuuumpa! (baggle baggle)

That is the noise Lumphy makes when he is in it, because he rides three-quarters of the way up the turning drum, then Fwuuumpa!

drops down to the bottom, onto TukTuk and

the clothes and

(baggle baggle)

bumps around a few times before riding up

the drum again.

It is not his favorite experience, at all.

In fact, he feels sick to his stomach worse than he's ever felt sick to his stomach before, but he keeps his mouth shut. He doesn't complain one tiny complaint, even. He is so happy that the Dryer is well again. That she won't be dragged off to the dump and replaced by a stranger.

That Frank will not be lonely.

That all the wishing on the stars

maybe

helped.

. . . . .

When the Dryer halts, it is after dinnertime, but the spring sky is still bright, the evening sun shining through the basement windows. Honey and her parents are out of the house. Lumphy can tell by how quiet it is.

"I am so glad you're feeling better," he calls, after the Dryer's drum rolls to a stop. She swings her door open, and since the house is empty, he climbs out. TukTuk remains in an exhausted heap with the Girl-clothes.

"We all wished and hoped that you'd be okay," Lumphy tells the Dryer. "We were so worried."

"*I* was so worried," puts in Frank. "With you pulled out from the wall like that—you can't even imagine. Sometimes I thought that workman didn't know what he was doing. I thought you were never going to tumble dry again. I thought you were leaving me." Frank sobs. "I was so lonely. I didn't know what to do!"

"There, there, love," says the Dryer. "I know. I know. But it's all right now."

. . . . .

Late at night, when the people are sound asleep, Lumphy creeps upstairs and gets Plastic, Sheep, StingRay, Spark, Bonkers, Millie, Brownie, and Rocky. They bring down jingle sticks, finger cymbals, a maraca, some silver confetti, and several orange and yellow balloons found in the bottom of the toy box. When they get to the basement, they sprinkle the floor with silver, then wake up Frank, the

Dryer, TukTuk, and the purple towels. Spark, who is hollow, blows up the balloons.

Dance party!

Frank starts off with "Love Train" and the towels join in, providing backbeat and harmonies. Rocky and Millie bounce on the towels, and Lumphy bangs the cymbals. StingRay taps her tail and, as the beat gets her going, begins hopping up and down with her flippers and leaping into the air.

"The party is for you, not just the Dryer," Lumphy tells TukTuk. "I won't forget to invite you again."

Frank overhears and interrupts "Love Train" to boom, "Shall I sing something for the little lady?"

"Yes, please," says Lumphy. "Because she is my particular towel friend." He rubs his buffalo nose against TukTuk's warm folds, and Frank improvises:

> "Tuk-itty TukTuk
> Yellow like a yellow duck

Tuk-itty TukTuk

Boom! (hey!)

Tuk-itty TukTuk

Yellow like a chicken cluck

Tuk-itty TukTuk

Boom!"

The song is so good, they sing it six times.

"Tuk-itty TukTuk

Yellow like a corn shuck

Tuk-itty TukTuk

Boom! (hey!)

TukTuk is yellow

Like a Caterpillar dump truck

Tuk-itty TukTuk

Boom!"

TukTuk, seated on top of the Dryer and singing backup with some other towels, isn't angry with Lumphy anymore. The music is loud. Plastic bounces and spins. Spark rears onto her tail and waggles a jingle stick ferociously, and StingRay is flapping and clapping. Lumphy is going to town with the cymbals. Bonkers and Brownie are wiggling themselves so hysterically, they keep falling over their tails, which sends them into fits of giggles, while the Dryer swings her front door open and shut and blinks all her lights on and off. She is dancing!

"Sweetheart," says Frank when the TukTuk song is over. "This next one's for you. Towels, back me up some more. Here we go!"

"She's our Dryer! La da dee dah!
And she's healthy! Deedle dee bah!
We love that Dryer!
(Shake, shake, and shake)

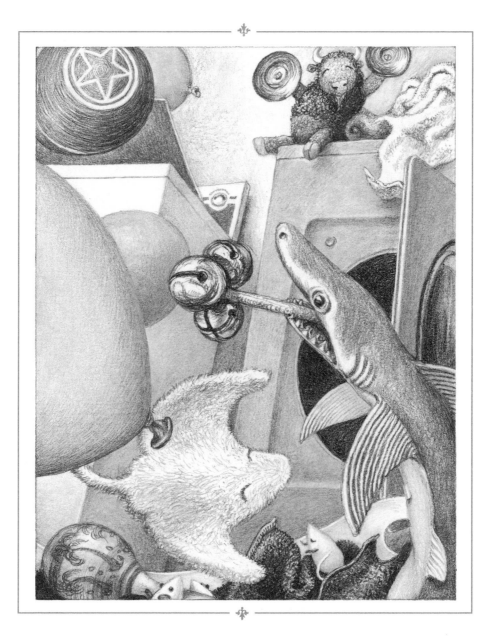

'Cause she's our Dryer!

(Shake, shake, and shake)

If you're damp, she'll dry you out,

If you're cold, she'll warm you up.

She makes a lovely rumble sound.

We're glad our Dryer's still around!

(Everybody now!)

She's our Dryer! La da dee dah!

And she's healthy! Deedle dee bah!

We love that Dryer!

(Shake, shake, and shake)

'Cause she's our Dryer!

(Shake, shake, and shake)

Oooooooooh, yeah!"

CHAPTER SIX

✤

Let's Do Our Nails

Plastic and Spark are in the bathtub. It is bouncy to have a friend to float with, and Plastic is boinging herself against the tiled wall and dropping back into the water with a big splash. Spark is swimming in circles with only her fin above the water. It is a Saturday afternoon in late spring. Honey has a soccer game, and the family is out of the house.

Lumphy watches Plastic and Spark from atop the

closed toilet seat, and StingRay is looking at the pretty colors of nail polish lined up at the back of the sink. Purple, red, pale green, and glitter gold. Robin's egg blue, even. Each one has a tiny brush inside for painting fingernails.

That robin's egg blue polish is almost the same color as StingRay herself.

Plop! Plastic boings into the water again.

"You're splashing too much," StingRay warns, waving a flipper. "See those water spots on my plush? And look at that puddle on the floor. How are we going to clean it all up?"

"Don't use *me*," warns TukTuk, from her place on the rack. "I only just dried out from last night, and for once I'm folded neatly."

"Calm down, people. We'll use the bath mat," says Spark, lifting her head out of the water.

The bath mat doesn't talk.

"A bath mat doesn't have the same absorbency as a

towel," says TukTuk. "You're not going to soak up that whole puddle with just a bath mat."

"I can get a purple towel from the grown-up bathroom," proposes Lumphy.

"Or Plastic could stop splashing," says StingRay. "If she weren't splashing, there wouldn't be a problem."

"Sorry." Plastic is embarrassed.

"Stop worrying," says Spark, lifting her head out again. "It's not like Honey's observant or anything. She won't notice a little water, and neither will her parents."

"Honey is, *too*, observant," says Plastic.

"Suit yourself." Spark heaves herself onto the ledge of the tub, dripping water onto the tiles. "But what kind of a kid leaves a shark in a box and then a mouse in a vacuum cleaner? Unobservant, that's what kind."

"She didn't *know* Bonkers got sucked into the vacuum!" cries StingRay.

"Because she failed to *observe it*," says Spark.

StingRay is loyal. "Honey's very busy. She's got soccer and chores and homework to think about."

"She's getting older," puts in Lumphy. "That's what the problem is."

"I'm just saying," Spark explains. "Honey forgot to get Lumphy out of the basement the night we had the dance party. She didn't play with you guys at the sleepover. Plus she's forcing me to play dress-up and do stupid Barbie stuff, when any kid paying attention should be able to tell I don't like it. Hello? Honey is okay, but she doesn't seem that into us, if you want to know what I think."

"She used to be wonderful," says Plastic. "Just wonderfully wonderful."

Plastic hates that Spark doesn't love Honey, because Plastic loves her no matter what and for always—but it is true that things are not quite the same as they were when Honey was younger.

"She didn't notice I had that hole in my flipper," StingRay admits.

"She doesn't play in the bath anymore," adds TukTuk.

"She didn't take us on vacation," says Lumphy. "Not one single one of us."

"And there's not as much specialness." This last is hard for StingRay to say. She looks at the floor while she speaks. "It used to seem like the specialness would go on forever and ever, but now it's hardly ever special."

Spark drops into the bathtub again, pulls the plug with her teeth, and hurls her rubbery body over the ledge onto the bath mat. She shakes herself dry like a dog and announces: "Let's do our nails."

"What?" asks Lumphy.

"Our nails. I see you checking out that polish, StingRay."

StingRay nods absently. She is still thinking about the specialness problem.

"Pretty, isn't it?" says Spark.

"I don't have any nails," says Plastic, nervous. "It's normal for a ball!"

"Neither do I," says Spark. "Who cares? 'Do our nails' is an expression. We'll paint something else with the nail polish. That'll cheer you guys up, won't it?"

Plastic bounces over to look at the colors. "Oooh!" she cries. "There's gold here! Real live glitter gold!"

"What would we paint instead of nails?" StingRay wonders. "The Barbie box or something?" The idea comes out of her mouth without any planning.

"Aha!" cries Spark.

"Aha what?"

"Aha, *yes*! The Barbie box!" Spark throws herself out the bathroom door and down the hall. "Fantastic idea, fishie!" she calls over her top fin.

Lumphy and StingRay look at one another for a minute, StingRay feeling surprised at the idea she has voiced. Painting the Barbie box.

She didn't mean to suggest it.

Or maybe she did.

In fact, she did mean it.

That stupid box and those silent Barbies, getting all the attention and specialness.

StingRay grabs two bottles of polish from the edge of the sink and leaps with them down to the floor. "What are you waiting for?" she asks Lumphy.

"Nothing," Lumphy answers. "I'm waiting for nothing." He scrambles up, sticks two bottles under his front legs, one more in his mouth—and jumps. The two of them hurry down the hall.

"Wait!" calls Plastic, unsure.

No answer.

"They're not waiting," says TukTuk.

Plastic calls again. "Are you doing a nice thing?" she asks. "Or a naughty thing?"

Silence.

"They're not listening, either," says TukTuk.

. . . . .

Lumphy and Spark drag the Barbie box to the center of Honey's bedroom. It is closed tight, with the Barbies and all their clothes inside. StingRay loosens the caps on the nail polish.

"You have to be very neat," Lumphy warns his friends. "Because Frank can't help you with nail polish."

"What about dry cleaning?" StingRay is anxious.

"That won't get polish out, either. TukTuk told me Honey's mother takes her nail color off with a special remover," Lumphy explains. "Plus, she keeps it in the medicine cabinet, which is hard to get to. So don't spill any polish on yourself or you'll never get clean."

StingRay begins with the robin's egg blue, which will match her plush even if she does spill. She is painting herself—a large and beautiful stingray—right over the picture of a Barbie doll on one end of the box.

StingRay makes the darling curve of her own tail, the strong arch of her flippers, the adorable shape of her own nose, loving the feel of the polish brush as it slides across the vinyl. Loving the blue. Loving, even, the smell of the polish.

Spark has been scribbling, holding the brush in her teeth and making violent slashes of light green. "I'm cheering up already," she says, out one corner of her mouth. "You cheering up, bison?"

Lumphy has made a thick red line all along the crack where the lid meets the rest of the box. It is a dark and angry scrawl, but he does like the look of the deep red against the soft pink of the box. He tells Spark, "Yes," and tries something: a flower. And another. And another. Then he changes colors and paints purple flowers.

Sheep rolls over to see what's happening. "Is that clover you're painting?" she asks the shark. "Or is it grass?"

"It's the ocean," says Spark.

"Oh." Sheep thinks for a minute or two and then asks, "Don't you think it would be good if you painted some clover? Then it would be interesting."

"Interesting to you, maybe."

"Everyone is interested in clover," says Sheep. "What's not to like?"

Spark doesn't answer. She's concentrating. Sheep watches a little longer, then tips over on her side and falls asleep.

· · · · ·

Plastic has been rolling herself dry on the bath mat, thinking. "I don't want to be naughty," she tells TukTuk. "I want to be nice."

"So be nice if you want to be nice," TukTuk says.

Plastic thinks some more. "Did you see that nail polish?" she asks.

Yes, TukTuk saw it.

"There was a glitter gold color."

"Um hm."

"Glittery goldy gold," says Plastic. "So so bright, glittery gold polish!"

"Are you changing your mind?" asks TukTuk. "Are you going to be naughty now?"

"I'm changing my mind!" yells Plastic, twirling. "Glittery goldy gold polish!"

She bounces down the hall after the others.

. . . . .

Everyone's paintings look excellent, thinks Plastic, bounding into the bedroom. "Glittery goldy gold!" she cries again. "Is anyone using it? Can I have a turn?"

StingRay pours a puddle of glitter gold on the big flat lid of the Barbie box.

"Thank you!" says Plastic, springing up. "Ooooh, it feels slippy! And sticky!"

Plastic rolls from side to side and round and round in the polish, coating the pink vinyl with gold. "Look at me!" she squeals, twisting herself in circles to create a spiral pattern in glitter. "I'm painting! I'm painting with no hands!"

Her painting is so swirly and goldy gold. Plastic hops off the box to let the others see what she's done, and rolls joyfully around on the rug, thinking only about gold and what a happy bright color it is.

"Don't come so close to me," snaps StingRay. "I'm dry clean only."

Plastic stops rolling.

"Uh-oh." Lumphy looks at Plastic and shakes his head.

"What?"

Lumphy coughs. "You're gold."

"I am?"

"And the carpet. It's gold, too."

Plastic looks around. Lumphy is right. She has left a sticky path of glitter gold everywhere she rolled.

"It doesn't come off," scolds Lumphy. "Weren't you listening when I explained?"

No. Plastic had been in the bathroom when he explained.

Oh no no no—Plastic has been so naughty! She has never been naughty like this before. What to do, what to do?

Before she has time to think, before anyone has time to think, the toys hear a key in the door.

The people are home early.

Rumpa lumpa

Rumpa lumpa

Frrrrrr, frrrrrr.

Grunk! Gru-GRUNK!

Lumphy, StingRay, and Spark hide beneath the high bed, tipping over two jars of polish as they run. But Plastic is scared to move. If she rolls or bounces, she'll track nail color on even more of Honey's carpet. What to do, what to do?

The parents come upstairs. The mother stops short when she sees the mess. "Honey?" she calls in a strained voice. "Can you come here now, please?"

The dad scratches his neck and speaks in a low, angry voice. "Look what she did to her rubber ball. And to the sheep. And the rug."

"And all that nail polish she just got," the mom adds. "And her Barbie box."

Honey enters the room and catches sight of Plastic, covered with glitter gold. And Sheep, asleep in a puddle of Spark's green polish. She walks over and looks at the

Barbie box, painted with a curious mix of ugly, angry scribbles and beautiful art.

Honey knows the toys have done it. Plastic can tell from her expression.

They have never done anything this bad before. Nothing that would get Honey in trouble.

Will she know why they did it? Will she be angry?

She pulls Plastic off the sticky carpet. She begins to lift Sheep, too, but as she does there is a ripping noise.

The noise of a felt ear—the only ear Sheep has left—tearing.

Part of Sheep's ear is stuck to the carpet with nail polish.

Honey's hand stops for a moment, but there is no other way to move Sheep. Gently, she rips the ear the rest of the way and holds the wounded Sheep in her arms. "I'm sorry," she says to her mom and dad. "It was a bad idea and I should have cleaned it up. I was careless."

Plastic nearly twitches with surprise and relief. Honey squeezes her.

"I'll clean off all my toys, and buy you new remover with my allowance," continues Honey. "I'll try to clean the carpet, too."

The mother shakes her head, still angry.

"It's a start," says the dad.

. . . . .

Honey takes Plastic, Sheep, and the Barbie box to the bathroom, where she rubs polish remover on Sheep's matted wool. Some of the polish comes off, but Sheep will be forever green around the left side of her neck and head. Her hearing—though not gone—will be worse than before. Honey puts a Band-Aid on the ear nub. She dabs Plastic with remover, then rinses the ball under the tap and dries her with TukTuk. The clumps of polish come off pretty easily, but it looks as though Plastic will remain shimmery, with a slight residue of glitter gold.

Plastic doesn't mind. Honey doesn't seem mad at all. She's taking care of them! She even squeezed Plastic in an understanding way. Besides, Plastic thinks, the glittery goldy gold looks *very* good.

When Plastic and Sheep are as clean as they can get, Honey looks at the paintings on the Barbie box. She tries to open it.

It won't open.

Honey runs a cotton ball dipped in remover along the edges, but Spark has put so much sticky green along her side of the box, and Lumphy so much red on his, that the lid won't separate from the bottom.

The Barbies are still inside.

Honey tugs and pulls—but the box won't open.

The Barbies will probably have to stay in there for a very, very long time, together with all their clothes.

Honey carries Plastic and Sheep and the ruined Barbie box into the bedroom, where she places the box on top of the bookshelf so everyone can see it. She finds Lumphy, StingRay, and Spark under the bed and sets them to-gether on the fringed pillows.

Lumphy's stomach feels awful, and StingRay's body is tight with anxiety. They peek at Spark, but it is impossible to tell what the shark is thinking.

Will Honey yell at them and give them time-outs in a bucket in the hallway? StingRay wonders.

Or send them off to the zoo to be teased by the real live animals?

Or leave them at the dump because she doesn't love them anymore?

"You sweetie guys," Honey announces. "This is the best present I ever got."

"We're not in trouble!" Plastic whispers to her friends.

"Even though you made a mess, and Sheep's ear got hurt," Honey continues, "I know you meant for it to be a surprise. The picture of StingRay is just the right blue, huh? And blue is the best color." She smiles at StingRay. "And here are the golden swirls, and these pretty flowers, and the greeny grass on the other side. You guys are big big sweeties to make this."

Spark's top fin twitches ever so slightly in annoyance.

Honey pats Sheep and strokes StingRay's tail. "I know I haven't played with you much lately." She pets Lumphy's woolly back. "But I love you. And I will always keep you," she swears. "StingRay, Plastic, and Lumphy. Sheep and DaisySparkle. Even Highlander and the mice. I'll keep all of you, forever."

. . . . .

"What did I tell you?" grumps Spark as soon as Honey has gone downstairs for dinner. "Un. Ob. Ser. Vant."

"We're not in trouble!" says Plastic, rolling a circle around her friends. "She loves us forever and she didn't mind that we were naughty!"

"She didn't even know we *were* naughty," says Spark. "She missed the entire point."

Lumphy sniffs. "She thought it was a present. It was the opposite of a present."

"Exactly." The shark twitches her tail and mutters: "Greeny grass. Hmph."

StingRay eyes the Barbie box. "It's stuck shut, isn't it?" she says, wonderingly. "They're not coming out again."

"Not for a good long while, anyway," says Spark. "At least we got that done."

"She loves us all!" cries Plastic.

"It's true," says StingRay, swishing her tail thoughtfully. "She did say that. But it still feels like not as much. Like she loves us—but *not as much* as she used to."

"But forever!" says Plastic.

"Yes," says StingRay. "Forever but not as much."

. . . . .

That night, after Honey has gone to sleep, Sheep has a tearless cry over her lost ear. And her green face. And Honey growing up. It is the first time in her long sheep-y life that she has ever cried. The sobs sound like this: "Herffle, herffle. Herffle, herffle."

Plastic feels sorry for Sheep, she really does, but it is hard for her to keep still and act sympathetic. Every few minutes she rolls down the hall to bounce in front of the bathroom mirror, admiring her beautiful new sheen. "I'm a gold ball, a gold ball!" she whispers to her reflection.

Lumphy understands how Sheep feels about her ear. He lost his tail a long time ago. Sometimes he still misses it. He nuzzles Sheep's face.

"Herffle, herffle. Herffle, herffle," she sobs.

Lumphy keeps nuzzling, but the herffles keep herffling.

"Should I tell a story?" asks StingRay. She lay down with Honey at eight-thirty, but after the events of the day found it impossible to fall asleep. Now she is on the carpet, worrying about her wounded friend. "Would it help to hear a story, so you can think about something else?"

Sheep nods.

StingRay taps her flippers for attention. Spark and the toy mice scootch across the carpet to listen.

StingRay thinks how nice it is to feel important and helpful. She is such a considerate and special stingray!

She is about to launch into the tale of Princess Daisy-Sparkle and the fairy treasure when she looks down at her friends and remembers: that is not Sheep's favorite story.

It is not Lumphy's, either.

The toy mice aren't very interested, and Spark positively dislikes it.

It is only StingRay's favorite story.

StingRay really *does* want to tell it, though.

And StingRay thinks the things that Sheep likes—are boring. It would be so much more interesting to tell about DaisySparkle.

"Herffle, herffle. Herffle, herffle," goes Sheep.

StingRay makes a decision. "Once upon a time, there was a meadow," she says loudly, making sure that Sheep can hear. "A wide grassy meadow with lots of juicy green clover.

Clover so bright it almost glowed.

There were goats and sheep and rabbits,

all living in the meadow.

The rabbits ate the clover,

and the goats ate the clover,

and do you know who else ate the clover?

The sheep! They ate as much clover

as ever they wanted, each day.

They ate grass, and there were, like,

four different kinds.

The sheep ate these, and when they wanted

dessert,

there were pretty flowers in the meadow

that were also good to eat."

StingRay talks into the night, boring but pretty stuff about greenery and chewing. As she talks, Sheep gradually stops herffling.

Highlander pricks his ears. Bonkers squirms and occasionally bites his own tail, while Brownie falls asleep on top of Millie and Rocky. Spark chews on a puzzle piece while she listens. Plastic, feeling gorgeous, rolls back into the bedroom and leans herself against Lumphy.

StingRay makes up stories, and she can tell it is helping.

The stars twinkle outside the window, and the toys cuddle up.

Everything is good again, because they are together.

A Note on the Textual References

The book about the mouse in the dungeon is *The Tale of Despereaux* by Kate DiCamillo. The TV show about the children who drink pink milk is *Charlie & Lola*, adapted from the picture books by Lauren Child: *I Will Never Not Ever Eat a Tomato*, *I Am Too Absolutely Small for School*, etc. The movie entitled *The Fairy Treasure* does not exist.

As Spark points out, Lumphy is an American buffalo, which is to say, he is technically a bison. American buffalo are not true buffalo (like the water buffalo of Asia or the cape buffalo of Africa—to whom they are only distantly related). Instead, they are most closely related to the European bison, and the species to which they belong is *bison*. However, Lumphy himself knows nothing about any of this.

"Love Train" is the 1973 hit by the O'Jays. I chose it as Frank's favorite song from the radio because I thought it would sound good in Frank's voice and because children I know enjoy it.

The nature documentaries described are imaginary, and the "facts" about great white sharks spurious. Likewise, the information about cheese.

Acknowledgments

Thank you, first, to all the children who wrote to me asking for a sequel to *Toys Go Out*, many of you sending paintings and drawings of the characters. I have loved getting your mail, and it inspired me as I worked on *Toy Dance Party*.

Thank you to Ivy for listening to lots of early drafts, inviting me to spontaneous dance parties, and giving me the idea of naming a rubber shark after a princess. Thanks to Daniel for asking if the washing machine talked, back when I was writing the first book—and for the rubber shark itself. And for being so patient when I had to write on our long-awaited vacation.

Griffin was the first person to shove garbage into our rubber shark, and I appreciate his ingenuity. Errolyn allowed her toy buffalo to be photographed for my school visits, and Heather took the picture. John and Maureen, my writing companions, helped me think of disgusting ingredients for pink milk. Scott was not there on the pink milk day, but he kept me on track by writing next to me as well, while Libba did the same during final revisions.

My debt and admiration to the incomparable Paul O.

Zelinsky for his art, advice, and enthusiasm. And for naming Spark, after I came up with DaisySparkle.

Enormous gratitude to Anne Schwartz for saying she'd publish a sequel if I wrote one, for editing me with a keen eye, and for waiting very patiently for me to be done with other stuff. I couldn't ask for better publishers than Anne and Lee Wade. Thanks also to Annie Kelly, Rachael Cole, Emily Seife, Adrienne Weintraub, Chip Gibson, Lisa Nadel, Lisa McClatchy, and Kathleen Dunn—plus everyone else who has worked so hard on my books at Random House.

About the Author

✤

Emily Jenkins is the author of several books for children and adults, including *Toys Go Out*, hailed as "ideal bedtime reading" by the *Wall Street Journal*; *Skunkdog*; *What Happens on Wednesdays*; and *That New Animal* and *Five Creatures*, each of which received a *Boston Globe–Horn Book* Honor. Ms. Jenkins lives in Brooklyn, New York. Visit her at www.emilyjenkins.com.

About the Illustrator

✤

Paul O. Zelinsky's retelling of the classic fairy tale, *Rapunzel*, was awarded the 1998 Caldecott Medal. He has also received three Caldecott honors, for *Hansel and Gretel*, *Rumpelstiltskin*, and *Swamp Angel*. Mr. Zelinsky is the creator of two pull-tab books: *The Wheels on the Bus* and *Knick-Knack Paddywhack!*, a *New York Times* Best Illustrated Book. His illustrations for *Toys Go Out* were called "charming . . . wonderfully detailed" by *Kirkus Reviews*. He lives in Brooklyn, New York. Visit him at www.paulozelinsky.com.